For a moment Leigh thought of inviting Christian in.

Then she decided against it. "Well, thanks for the ride," she said, opening the door and hopping out.

"I'll wait till you get in."

Leigh flashed him one last smile. "Thanks."

As she hurried up the walk to her house she ran her thumb over her fingertips. She knew it wasn't her imagination that Christian's fingers had lingered just a little too long on hers. Not that fingertips were the sexiest body part or anything, but it was the *way* he'd touched her. . . .

Opening the screen door, Leigh's eyes filled with sudden tears. How could she be so shameful? How could *she*, of all people, even want to touch Christian Archer's fingertips, especially after what had happened to Kerry's plans for a romantic evening? After she'd vowed only minutes earlier to write him off?

And how could she go on pretending things were normal now that she had?

84

Hard to Resist

Wendy Loggia

BANTAM BOOKS

NEW YORK · TORONTO · LONDON · SYDNEY · AUCKLAND

RL 6, age 12 and up

HARD TO RESIST

A Bantam Book / October 1998

*Produced by 17th Street Productions,
a division of Daniel Weiss Associates, Inc.
33 West 17th Street
New York, NY 10011.
Cover photography by Michael Segal.*

ISBN: 0-553-49253-5

Published simultaneously in the United States and Canada

*Bantam Books are published by Bantam Books, a division of Bantam
Doubleday Dell Publishing Group, Inc. Its trademark, consisting of the
words "Bantam Books" and the portrayal of a rooster, is Registered in
U.S. Patent and Trademark Office and in other countries. Marca
Registrada. Bantam Books, 1540 Broadway, New York, New York 10036.*

PRINTED IN THE UNITED STATES OF AMERICA

OPM   0 9 8 7 6 5 4 3 2 1

*To the very special little someone who came
into existence as I wrote this book.*

*And many thanks to my editor,
Raina Korman.*

One

"DON'T EVEN TELL me that was the last one."
Leigh Feralano shot her best friend, Kerry Cole, a guilty look as she licked the gooey chocolate residue from her fingertips. "Okay, I won't."

"Leigh!" Kerry went for the crumpled Cookie Emporium bag. "I wanted the one with the macadamia nuts and white chocolate," she wailed, peering inside the empty sack. She put her hand on her forehead. "Oh, no. I feel hot. Maybe I'm getting sick. Maybe that cookie was the last thing that would have kept me from passing out from sugar deficiency."

Leigh giggled as they walked down the wide, air-conditioned colonnade of the Walden Galleria, the largest mall in Buffalo. The late August heat was unbearable, and tons of people were taking refuge inside the cool, store-lined corridors. "Uh, I think you're forgetting the Häagen-Dazs frozen chocolate bars we had an hour ago."

1

"Well . . ."

"And the lemonade and hot pretzels."

"If you're going to count *those* . . . ," Kerry said, tossing the bag into a garbage bin.

Leigh wrinkled her nose. "Count? I refuse to do that until I slide into one of Mr. Franklin's cramped wooden desks while he passes out crummy used math textbooks." She smoothed back the long dark strands of hair that had loosened from her ponytail and sighed. This summer, her first one in Buffalo and one of the best of her life, was over way too fast. "I can't believe I've lived here a whole year already."

Kerry grinned. "And I can't believe that tomorrow is, well, tomorrow!" She checked her watch and tapped its face with a peach-colored nail. "In exactly twenty-eight hours and sixteen minutes, Christian will be home!"

Christian. Kerry's boyfriend. The boyfriend that Leigh had never met. Leigh couldn't stop a million questions and worries from buzzing through her brain at the mention of his name. Would he really be as funny and charming as Kerry always said he was? Would he like her or think she was a dork? And most important, would Kerry still have time to hang out with Leigh once he was home?

"I can't wait to see him!" Kerry exclaimed.

Snapping out of her thoughts, Leigh pushed her concerns to the back of her mind and tried to concentrate on being happy for her best friend. "Too bad you're not excited or anything," she teased halfheartedly.

"Christian's been in that study abroad program in England for a whole year," Kerry responded. "I've never been so excited to see someone in my whole life!"

Yup, Leigh thought miserably as she watched Kerry continue to beam, *I'm going to take the backseat to Christian in a major way.* Then she forced a smile. "Well, it's a good thing that he's finally coming back because I was starting to think he was some figment of your overactive romantic imagination."

Kerry sniffed. "There's no way I could dream up a boy as perfect as Christian." Her mouth formed into a worried frown. "I only hope that he'll be as happy to see me as I'm going to be to see him."

"I'm sure he will be," Leigh assured her. "You guys have been together for such a long time—he loves you."

"You're right." Kerry smiled brightly again. "I just want our reunion to go as smoothly as possible."

"Well, let's see. In preparation for King Christian's return you talked your mom into letting you get your hair cut at the swankiest salon in town, we gave each other hot oil manicures, your skin is zit free, and even though you've eaten enough junk food to summon the diet police, you still look like a supermodel." Leigh put her hands on her hips. "Did I leave anything out?"

"A new outfit?"

Leigh slapped herself lightly on the forehead. "Of course."

"I've got to find something really cool to wear to the airport," Kerry said as they walked into Express. "Maybe a cute pair of jeans. Or a halter top and some shorts. Or maybe I should dress up. . . ."

"You'll look great in whatever you pick out," Leigh assured her. "And once Christian sees that gorgeous face of yours, what you have on won't matter."

Kerry came to a dead stop in between a rack of pants and tank tops. "I'm really going to see him tomorrow, aren't I?" she whispered, looking to Leigh for confirmation.

Leigh nodded. "Looks that way." She smiled at Kerry as she tried to fight the anxiety that began to wash over her again.

Leigh knew the truth was that tomorrow, once Christian was back, life as she knew it would be over: No more half-mile bike rides to 7-Eleven just to get a cherry Slurpee. No more two-hour giggle-filled phone conversations. And definitely no more Saturday nights renting sad romances or gory horror movies and pigging out on double-cheese pizza and Doritos.

Tomorrow. The day that would change everything.

The day Christian Archer was coming home.

"Is it me?" Kerry asked, holding up a skirt so short, it should have been X-rated.

"Well, it's not me." Leigh frowned. "And I'm not sure it should be you." Leigh was more of a flannel boxers and T-shirt kind of person.

"Nah, maybe not." Kerry's eyes lit on a strappy

4

black dress. "Now that, on the other hand, could definitely be me." She handed Leigh her purse and the shopping bag containing the new Levi's she'd just bought. "Hold this while I try it on, okay?"

Leigh nodded and dropped down into one of the cool leather chairs usually occupied by girls' boyfriends, sighing heavily. The anxious feeling in the gut of her stomach hadn't gone away. It had gotten worse.

Ever since Leigh had met Kerry, she'd known about Christian and that he'd be coming home one day. But it had all seemed so distant. Christian never existed for Leigh in person—he was just a vague someone who Kerry talked about. But now what? Would her relationship with Kerry be the same once Christian was here in the flesh?

Leigh fidgeted with the handle on the shopping bag. It wouldn't be so bad if she had a boyfriend too.

Yeah, right. Like that was going to happen. She'd been sure that when she moved to Buffalo, there'd be some great guy who'd sweep her off her feet. But the cute guys all seemed to be taken or stuck-up, and the not-so-cute guys made for good friends, but they didn't make her heart thump or anything.

"What do you think?" Kerry came out of the dressing room and did a slow twirl. The knit fabric hugged her body perfectly, the open back just low enough to make any guy look twice.

"You look great," Leigh said. She slumped back

into the chair. "Too great." Suddenly she found herself fighting back tears. It was all too much.

Kerry's face fell. "Leigh, what's wrong?"

"Nothing," Leigh lied, picking at the seam of the chair. But she knew exactly what it was. Leigh knew she was being rotten and petty, but she couldn't help herself. "I'm sorry, Ker. I just . . . I just . . ." Her chin began to quiver. "I don't want to lose you," she said in a small voice.

"Lose me? What are you talking about?"

Leigh shrugged. "When Christian comes back, you guys are going to want to be together a lot, and I—I'm going to miss you, that's all." She tried to laugh, but all that came out was a tiny, hollow cough.

"That is the dumbest thing I've ever heard."

"No, it's not."

"Yes, it is." Kerry went back in the dressing room, shutting the wooden half door behind her. "I *am* capable of having a boyfriend and friends, you know. Kind of like chewing gum and walking at the same time."

Leigh scuffed her toe along the gray carpet of the waiting area.

"Things won't change," Kerry insisted. "You and I are going to hang out all the time. And who knows?" she said, coming out of the dressing room with the dress draped over her arm. "Maybe this year you'll meet someone too."

"Maybe," Leigh said halfheartedly.

"And that garbage about losing me?" Kerry gave

Leigh a hug. "In case you forgot, you're my best friend. That's never going to change!"

Leigh smiled weakly and hugged her friend back. "You're right."

But in her heart of hearts, Leigh didn't believe it. Guys always changed things. Always.

TWO

"ANOTHER SATURDAY NIGHT alone? If the answer is yes, it's time to call 1-900-PARTNER, the guaranteed way to meet your match. Why are you waiting? Just pick up the phone and—"

With a sigh Leigh turned off the TV and trudged out to the kitchen. Her dad was pouring himself a glass of milk.

"Hey, Dad."

He smiled over at her. "You sound like I feel. Everything okay?"

"Just bored."

"Want to help me? I'm working on a model." Leigh's dad was a seismologist. Buffalo had one of the best earthquake research centers in the world, which was why they'd moved there in the first place.

"No thanks." Leigh grabbed a bag of Milano cookies. "I should probably get a head start on my summer reading list."

Mr. Feralano looked at the calendar. "Are you sure? You still have two days left."

"Funny," Leigh called over her shoulder, returning to the family room and plopping down on the couch. But as she sat there and tried to read, she couldn't concentrate. When the telephone rang, she jumped up to answer it. "Hello?"

"Get over here, fast!"

"Kerry?"

"What?" Kerry's voice sounded faint and breathy, like she'd been laughing really hard.

"No. I mean, I just wasn't sure it was you. You sound different," Leigh said.

"Like I'm in *luv?*" Kerry crooned.

"Uh, yeah. I guess so. So what's up?" She could hear loud music and muffled voices in the background.

"Well, Christian and I were just kind of planning to hang out alone tonight, right? But then Tim and his obnoxious little friends wanted to talk to him, and then my parents joined in, and so did Jason Minot and some other guys from school, and it ended up being a spur-of-the-moment party kind of thing," she finished in one big gulp. "You have to come over."

"Tonight?"

"No, next Friday. Of course tonight!" Kerry burst out. "Come on, Leigh."

Leigh hesitated. She *was* dying to meet Christian, but was she ready to witness their coupledom so soon? They'd probably be staring into each other's

9

eyes lovingly all night and laughing about old private jokes that Leigh could never take any part in.

"Do you have something better to do?" Kerry prompted.

Leigh picked a cookie crumb off her sweatshirt, stalling for time. "Well, um, no, not really."

"Good. You're really going to like him. I promise. Okay?"

"Okay," Leigh said at last.

"Gotta go. I can't wait for you to get here! Bye!"

Leigh stood there for a few minutes, clutching the phone. Then she realized that moping around wasn't going to get her anywhere. In fact, it was a totally wimpy thing to do. Christian was back and Kerry was happy, and Leigh was going to have to learn to deal.

Besides, she thought, trying to look on the bright side, *you can ask Christian all about what it was like to live and travel throughout England.* Ever since Leigh had watched a documentary on the Tower of London five years ago, she'd been fascinated by everything English: the high drama of the British royal family, ultracool London fashion, all the awesome rock bands and hilarious British movies. . . . What wasn't there to love?

But just because Christian had picked the hippest place on the planet to study in didn't necessarily mean she was going to find him easy to talk to. No, based on how Kerry had described him, he'd probably be so good-looking and cool that Leigh would be completely intimidated by him.

What *would* he be like?

Time to find out.

After her father agreed to drive her to Kerry's, Leigh took a quick shower and put on her red sweater and matching short plaid skirt with her new navy blue Dr. Martens. Then she gave her hair a quick brushing before dashing down the stairs.

Kerry's house was about ten minutes from Leigh's. Kerry lived near the university, on a tree-lined block with large, sturdy Tudors and freshly painted Colonials. Everyone had nicely manicured lawns and neatly trimmed hedges. A few of the trees had started to turn—rich ambers and oranges that made Leigh smile. She'd never been able to enjoy autumn in California, where everything looked the same whether it was May or October. Here things were different. Seasons changed, and they let you know it.

The Coles' driveway was filled with cars. Mr. Feralano pulled his Honda Accord up to the curb. "Call me when you're ready to leave."

Leigh leaned over and pecked his cheek. "I will, Dad." She hopped out of the car and hurried up the walk. Maybe she was being ridiculous, but she couldn't help it; she was nervous. After a year of feeling like a part of Kerry's family, right now all Leigh felt like was an outsider—as if Kerry and Christian's being together somehow eliminated the past twelve months of friendship she'd shared with Kerry.

Leigh straightened her skirt self-consciously and rang the bell. Maybe she should have just stuck with jeans. Did the skirt make her look fat? Maybe she—

Whish! The door flew open, startling her. "Oh, it's you. I thought it was the pizza guy." Kerry's not-so-charming thirteen-year-old brother, Tim, made a face at her.

"Good to see you too," Leigh said, laughing as she pushed past him. She couldn't believe how many people were there. They were everywhere: sitting on the steps that led outside, dancing in the living room, standing in huddled masses in the hallway. Tim's friends were sprawled out in the living room, surrounded by bowls of chips and pretzels, ogling the high-school guys who stood around talking sports. Leigh recognized the Dahlgrens, Kerry's next-door neighbors, helping to pour sodas in the kitchen. And there was Kerry, her head tilted back in laughter.

Leigh started toward her, then stopped short, her soles squeaking on the gleaming wood floor.

Standing in the center of the living room was the most gorgeous guy Leigh had ever laid eyes on. Dark, wavy brown hair that ended in a mass of curls at the nape of a soft neck. Hazel eyes that crinkled and laughed. A wonderful, warm, melt-in-your-mouth smile.

Who is he? Leigh wondered, her pulse racing. *Maybe Kerry was right. Maybe this* will *be the year I fall in love.*

Then Leigh watched as he took a couple of steps . . . and squeezed Kerry's shoulder.

This was Christian Archer.

With a sinking heart, Leigh realized she should've

recognized him from the pictures Kerry had plastered all over her room. Kerry and Christian at the prom, holding hands. Mugging for the camera at a Fourth of July picnic. Christian waving good-bye as he boarded the plane to London.

But he looked so different in person, in the all-too-incredible flesh.

He was wearing faded khakis with a tiny rip just below the knee, scuffed loafers without socks, and a washed-out-looking plaid shirt. Even though the shirt was cut large, it managed to reveal lean, muscular arms.

"Leigh!" Kerry squealed, pushing past a group of people. She hugged her. "Is he hot or what?"

"Definitely hot," Leigh whispered hoarsely, swallowing back the lump that had unexpectedly formed in her throat.

"Christian!" Kerry motioned excitedly for him to join them. Leigh watched as he threaded his way through the room, stopping to say hi to a few people on the way. Instinctively she lifted her hand to her neck and began to finger the silver spoon ring that dangled from her thin silver chain. Her grandma had given the ring to her for her twelfth Christmas and had died the following spring; Leigh hadn't taken it off since. She used the ring's smooth, familiar surface to calm her nerves.

And right now she was knee-weakeningly nervous.

"You've even got my third-grade teacher here!" Christian kidded Kerry as he reached them.

"Allow me to introduce my partner in crime, Leigh

Feralano," Kerry said, giving Leigh's arm a squeeze.

Christian stuck out his hand. "Nice to meet you."

"Hi." Leigh touched his palm with hers. His hand felt warm and firm. Hers felt soft and sweaty. A little sliver of electricity shot through her arm. "I'm so glad to finally see you in person," she said. "Welcome home."

"I hear you guys had a cool summer despite my absence," Christian joked. His soft hazel eyes twinkled down at her.

Leigh giggled. "We tried."

"Somebody had to keep me company when you left," Kerry protested, a fake pout on her lips. Then her smile flashed wide as a slow, smooth ballad swooned out from the CD player. "I love this song."

Leigh started to back up as Kerry slipped her arms around Christian's neck. "Well," she said, smiling awkwardly, "it was nice to meet—"

"The pizza and wings are here, Kerry!" Tim hollered, shoving in between Kerry and Christian. "Mom said you have to help her set up the food."

Kerry shot Tim a withering look. "Heaven forbid that *you* help out with anything around this place." She pecked Christian on the cheek, then turned to Leigh. "Be right back. Step in for me."

Leigh's eyes widened. "I don't think Christian wants to dance with me," she said in a low, panicky voice. She'd never slow danced with anyone, and she wasn't about to do it for the first time here, in the Coles' living room.

14

"Sure, he does!" Kerry grinned. "And I know how much you *love* to boogie."

Leigh wanted to throttle her. Kerry was always trying to get her to do things she wouldn't normally do: join the pep squad, talk to total strangers in the library, run for student council.

Dance with irresistibly cute guys that belong to other girls. Nope, this was a new one.

Christian held out his arm. "I'm no Fred Astaire, but . . ." He smiled tentatively.

"We, uh, we don't have to dance," she stammered, trying to fight back the blush that was racing to her cheeks.

"No, I'd like to."

Leigh took a deep breath as Christian gently pulled her close, his arms slipping around her waist. At five-foot four, she was a few inches shorter than he was, making it easy to avoid his gaze. She knew he was just trying to be polite, and the thought of him feeling sorry for her made her blush even more.

"It's funny," Christian said, interrupting her thoughts. "Some of the songs that are popular here now were big last year in England."

"Really?" Leigh said, trying not to look as flustered as she felt. There were so many questions she'd wanted to ask Christian, but now that she had the opportunity to talk to him, she was all tongue-tied. "You're so lucky to have gone there."

"I was half worried everyone would forget about me."

15

"Oh, no." Leigh shook her head. "I've heard about you every day for months."

"Must've been pretty painful." Christian grinned down at her.

"Only mildly." She smiled. "Really, though, I've been dying to meet you to see if you'd live up to Kerry's hype."

"And?"

"Except for the fact that you don't walk on air, you pretty much check out."

They both laughed and continued to sway back and forth to the music. Leigh tried to relax, but just when she would start to feel comfortable, she'd notice Christian's breath on her cheek or become suddenly aware of the light pressure of his hands on her back, and she'd get all nervous again.

It would be so great to dance with someone I was really into, Leigh thought dreamily, half closing her eyes. *It must be the best feeling in the world.*

"Hey, welcome home, Archer!" Christian and Leigh broke apart as some guys from school came over. They slapped Christian on the back as they greeted him.

"Just in time!" Kerry chimed in from behind. She handed Leigh a can of soda and a slice of pizza. "So what do you think?" she asked eagerly, popping a piece of pepperoni in her mouth.

"He's incredible," Leigh told her, meaning it more than she'd ever expected she would. Finally Leigh understood what Kerry had meant all those times when she spoke of Christian. He *was* special.

16

"I guess I'm pretty lucky." Kerry smiled and then moved forward to be near Christian.

Leigh leaned against the doorway and bit into her piece of soggy cheese pizza. Lucky seemed like an understatement. Blessed, favored, kissed by the gods . . . that was more like it. If the few minutes she'd just spent with Christian were any indication, Kerry had won the jackpot: He was terrific, and Leigh had never seen Kerry so happy.

For the millionth time in her fifteen years, Leigh wondered what it would be like to feel that way. To be in love.

Three

"OKAY," CHRISTIAN MUTTERED, rummaging through his frayed backpack as he jogged down the stairs Tuesday morning. "Notebooks, pens, class schedule . . ." He caught a glimpse of himself as he rounded the mirrored dining-room wall: semifaded jeans, slightly loose V-necked shirt, trainers he'd bought in England, hair reasonably under control . . . perfect. You definitely didn't want to look like you were trying too hard on the first day of school.

Christian bounded into the kitchen. His mom looked up from her glass of grapefruit juice and smiled over her morning paper. "Hi, sweetie."

Beth Archer had quit her job as a legal secretary several years ago to stay home and spend more time with her kids. Christian's English host mother, Julia, had been really nice, but with her coarse, graying hair, sensible shoes, and reserved sense of humor, she couldn't compare to his real mom.

"Hi." Christian grabbed a banana from the fruit bowl and joined his mom at the table. He'd never really thought about the fact that she always stocked up on fresh fruit and kept a not-so-secret hidden supply of cashews and chips in the bottom cupboard. Being alone in a foreign country had taught him a lot about appreciation. "Where's Em?"

His mother leaned forward. "She can't decide what shoes to wear."

"Do shoes matter when you're eight?" Christian asked.

"What doesn't matter when you're eight?"

Christian peeled back the banana, then stopped. His mother wore the goofiest expression on her face. "What? Do I have a big zit on my nose or something?"

Beth Archer laughed, shaking her head. "I just can't believe how handsome you've become. And that you're going to be a senior. Where have the years gone?"

"Mom." Christian gave his mother a kiss on the cheek. "Don't get all sentimental on me. Didn't you give me enough of that the other night?" His mom had cried more when he returned than when he'd actually left.

"A mom's allowed to be a little mushy if she wants to. Kerry's not the only one who can shed a few tears over you."

Kerry. Christian took a big bite of banana and checked his watch. He'd promised to pick her up by

19

eight o'clock, and it was already five to. After a year without dealing with the ups and downs of having a girlfriend, it felt a little weird to be someone's boyfriend again.

Kerry had come to the airport to greet him with his parents and Emily and a bunch of his friends. Hearing American voices, seeing his family and friends, passing by all the familiar places on his way home, the fact that he *was* home, took a while to sink in.

Everything had felt a little off, a little strange. Only now was he finally beginning to settle back in, to become Christian Archer, senior at Fillmore High. Son of Beth and Davis. Big brother to Emily. Soccer star hopeful. Guitar player. Art lover.

Kerry Cole's boyfriend.

His mother brushed his cheek with her hand, startling him. "Honey, is everything okay?"

"Sure. Why wouldn't it be?"

She took a sip of juice. "I don't know. It's just—well—" She paused. "Your relationship with Kerry is your own business, Christian. And Dad and I love her. You know that."

Christian nodded.

"But you two spent so much time together before you left, and I guess we hoped now that you're back, you wouldn't let yourself get tied down. It's just that . . ." She paused, her finger circling the glass's rim. "You're seventeen, Christian. Dad and I want to make sure that you don't get too serious."

Christian slung an extra banana in his backpack, wiped his mouth with a napkin, and pushed back his chair. It was cute how his mom was concerned. But she didn't need to be. Having a girlfriend like Kerry wasn't going to tie him down. Being with her was going to lift him up, make him feel good about himself, about life. That's how it had always been with Kerry. "Don't worry about that," he said.

"We're not trying to butt in," his mom added.

"I know." He smiled down at her. "See you later."

Just then Emily danced into the room, her long brown braid bouncing as she moved. "I'm going to be in third grade," she trilled.

Christian still couldn't believe how the little pip-squeak had grown. "Love those shoes, Em." Christian winked as he unlocked the back door. Her small dimpled face lit up with pride.

The keys to his dad's Chrysler in his hand, Christian opened the car door, slid behind the wheel, and headed toward Kerry's.

"Would you look at my hair?" Leigh moaned Tuesday morning, peering into the oval-shaped mirror that hung inside her chipped gold metal locker, G-601. Today was only the first day of school, but Leigh had already managed to give her locker a personality. Besides the mirror, she had covered the bottom of the locker with a square of magenta fur, taped pictures of her favorite male actors to the back wall, and stuck her collection of frog magnets on the door. It was still a locker, but at least it was a fashionable one.

Kerry leaned against G-602 and G-603 and gave each lock a spin. "You look good."

"You're not just saying that to hurry me up?" Leigh carefully dabbed some concealer on a zit that had the nerve to pop up on her chin.

"I would never lie about something as important as that," Kerry promised. She shifted her weight from one foot to the other. "But if you don't hurry, we're gonna be late, and I don't want to get one of Madame's squinty looks on the first day of school."

"Okay, okay, just a sec." Leigh stood on tiptoe and peered onto her top shelf to look for her copy of *Wuthering Heights,* their summer reading.

The occupant of G-603 appeared, and Kerry moved to Leigh's other side. "Any day now."

Spotting the novel, Leigh grabbed it along with her sack lunch and slammed the locker shut, tossing the tube of concealer back in her bag. "Do you know how many times I've had to wait for you while you—"

"Hey, Col-lano!" Petite, auburn-haired Lucy Evanczik and tall, spiral-curled Allison Wygate hurried over from the other side of the hall.

Leigh and Kerry grinned. "Hey, Zik-gate!" they cried in unison. The four girls were a steady foursome in the cafeteria last year and in lots of social events at FHS.

"Can you believe we're back in this place?" Allison asked, giving the hallway a disgusted eye roll.

"Summer flew," Kerry agreed.

"And how." Lucy lowered her voice. "Can you believe how cute Daryl Miller got? I just about *died* when I saw him." She glanced down the hall, and her jaw dropped. "Don't tell me that's Paul Kling. Oh. My. God."

"I see the hot summer sun didn't dry up your raging hormones or anything," Leigh said with a laugh. Lucy was notorious for developing monster crushes that lasted for about forty-eight hours.

Lucy nodded. "Time to fly," she said, yanking Allison's arm and heading down the hallway to follow Paul.

Leigh and Kerry slung their backpacks over their shoulders and began to make their way down the crowded hall. It was the usual back-to-school craziness: Worried-looking freshmen—the butt of many a junior and senior's jokes—were trying to look cool even though they were helplessly lost. Upperclassmen were busy catching up with old friends. And teachers seemed perfectly at home as they resumed ordering students out of the halls between classes and assigning monster homework.

"They're so into each other," Kerry said under her breath as they passed seniors Celia Shay and Steven Banks, tongue wrestling like crazy.

Leigh snuck a peek. "A little too much, huh?"

"Yeah, but if you're the one getting kissed like that, it's not so bad." Kerry's brow puckered with anxiety. "Leigh?"

"Hmmm?"

"Did you think that Christian looked, um, interested in me the other night? At my party?"

Leigh shot her a puzzled look. "The guy was glued to your side."

23

"I guess. I mean, I had a really good time, but it was also kind of strange," she said. "All this time I've been dying for Christian to come home, and now he's here, but I feel kind of funny when I'm around him. Like when he picked me up for school this morning, I wasn't quite sure what to say or how to act. It's so weird."

"I think that's completely normal."

"You do?"

"Sure. A lot of time has passed since you guys last saw each other. He was a junior, and now he's a senior. And you were a sophomore, and now you're a junior." Leigh raised a perfectly sculpted eyebrow. "That's a big difference."

"True."

"But you guys did e-mail each other all the time too," Leigh went on. "It's not like you haven't been part of each other's lives for the past year. Things will get back to normal again soon."

Kerry nodded. "But he shared his e-mail address with his host family. I didn't want to get too personal in the stuff I wrote. Who knew who was reading it?" She kicked a balled-up piece of paper down the hallway. "Besides, e-mail is one thing. Being together is another. I just"—she lowered her voice—"hope we fit together like we used to. That's all."

Leigh gave Kerry a reassuring pat on the back as they pushed open the creaky wooden door that led to their French class. *"Amour toujours amour,"* she whispered in Kerry's ear, managing to say something encouraging *and* keep Madame Josephine's long-standing rule of speaking only French in the classroom at the same time.

"You know I'm lousy at French," Kerry hissed.

"Love is always love," Leigh translated under her breath. She was the first to admit that she didn't have all the answers, but she knew one thing. Real-life love—the kind of love she hoped and dreamed was possible—never just went away or shriveled up and died because you were separated.

True love lasted forever.

"Okay, people. Settle down. Let's get started here." A tall blond woman wearing a short green dress rapped her knuckles on the desk at the front of the room.

"Finally," Kerry whispered from her seat next to Leigh. "A class that we're *all* together in." She leaned on Christian's desk behind her, smiling at him and Jason Minot.

Tall, gangly Jason was a senior and one of Christian's best friends. Leigh had gotten to know him through Kerry over the past year. Kerry had hoped that the two of them would hook up, but Leigh was content to just be friends with him. She could always count on Jason for a funny joke, and he could always count on her for help with his English papers.

Besides this morning's French class Leigh and Kerry had this health class twice a week, Tuesdays and Thursdays. They also had gym together on Mondays, Wednesdays, and Fridays. To their collective dismay, though, gym period was from 9:25

to 10:05, ruining any chances of looking good for the rest of the day.

"I had swimming first period." Christian pointed to his hair. "Guess I look kinda crazy, huh?"

"You look cute and you know it," Kerry teased.

Out of the corner of her eye Leigh took in his glossy dark waves, his thick curly eyelashes, piercing dimples, and white, even teeth.

Chlorine suited him.

"I can't believe my schedule this year," Jason griped behind Leigh, his long legs taking up a good three feet of aisle space.

"Me either. I guess I got spoiled with the variety of classes they offered at Lellington," Christian said.

Leigh wondered what kind of subjects Christian had studied at his school in England. She hadn't spoken to him much about his trip, but Leigh imagined that his classes must have been pretty cool. She knew he'd taken an art appreciation course and a British history course, both of which sounded way more interesting than the American Studies I and Math Course III classes that she was signed up for.

Screech. Leigh winced as the teacher's long red nails ran down the blackboard in an attempt to gain control of the chatting students. Several people groaned. A few girls screamed. And everyone stopped talking.

"Good. Works every time," the woman said, smiling. "I'm Mrs. Duncan. This is Teenage Health and Awareness, Tuesday, period five. Everyone in the right place?"

Twenty-six jaded heads went up and down.

"Okay. I'm going to pass around a sheet. Please print your name, whether you're a junior or senior, and fill in your home phone number and any topics you want covered this semester. If I can, I'll try to include as many of your ideas as possible."

"Is 'how to have sex in the school parking lot without being caught' a possibility?" muttered a kid with stringy, long brown hair in a Megadeth T-shirt.

Mrs. Duncan didn't flinch. "What about 'if you have sex in the school parking lot, you may end up with one of these,'" she said, holding up a doll.

"A doll?" Kerry blurted out.

"A baby." Mrs. Duncan smiled. "I'm thrilled to announce that our program received some additional funding over the summer, and as a result you'll all be participating in a wonderful educational experience. It's called Baby Think It Over."

"Maybe I should think over taking this class," the kid in the Megadeth shirt mumbled.

A few people started to laugh.

Mrs. Duncan smiled again. "I know it sounds funny. But teenage pregnancy is a serious issue." She lowered her voice. "Don't let the other teachers in the school know, but I think that this is probably the most important class you'll ever take." She looked around the room to make sure everyone was listening.

"The statistics on teenage pregnancy are astounding. Thousands of teenage girls become pregnant each year, and thousands of teenage boys become fathers. If we say this class is a standard representation of the national teenage population . . ."

Mrs. Duncan began rattling through a list of sobering statistics. Then she showed the class a video about teenage parents, featuring the teens themselves and their babies. Leigh had heard lots of the stats before, but actually seeing the people behind them made the subject a whole lot realer.

"Now, I'm sending home information packets about the program that I want you to give your parents to read and permission slips that I'd like them to sign," Mrs. Duncan explained as she rewound the tape. "You'll be divided into teams of two and assigned infant simulators to watch over for four days, beginning Thursday."

"You mean we've got to take the dolls home with us?" a guy on Leigh's right complained.

"And to school, and to football games, and to the mall, and wherever else you go," Mrs. Duncan stated, distributing the packets. "The dolls are programmed to cry at random intervals. Just like with a real baby, you won't know what's wrong, and you'll need to put your social life on hold, just like real moms and dads do." The teacher sat down on her desk. "This project is designed to help you make responsible choices and to learn what it's like to have a baby."

"My sister had a baby last year," Becky Salpone volunteered. "She's seventeen."

"Then I'm sure you realize that it's not easy," Mrs. Duncan said.

Becky nodded. "She has *no* life."

Mrs. Duncan put her hands on the desk and

28

leaned back. "Well, you all have a lot of life ahead of you, and I hope that this program helps you to see that being a mom or dad at your age is a lot more than having something cute and cuddly to play with." She pulled out her class roster. "I've taken the liberty of pairing you up, boys with girls."

Leigh glanced at the faces around her, hoping to spot a new or improved guy to be paired with. But there wasn't anybody she was really interested in. *Well, at least if there aren't any romantic possibilities, maybe Jason and I will end up together.*

Mrs. Duncan was announcing the pairs. "—Kerry Cole and Jason Minot, Sophia Mead and Will Kryski, Leigh Feralano and Christian Archer, Paula Greer and . . ."

I'm paired with Christian? Leigh turned back and gave him a tiny, self-conscious smile.

Kerry sighed heavily. "Why couldn't she have let us pick our own partners?"

"Gee, thanks a lot," Jason said, then pretended to cry.

Kerry socked him on the arm. "Oh, grow up."

Christian tossed his eraser from hand to hand. "What were the chances of us all being paired to-gether, huh?" He lowered his voice. "Things could be worse, Ker—you could have ended up with Metalhead over there."

Leigh giggled. "I've got an idea," she said, trying to cheer Kerry up. "Maybe I could switch with you."

"—there you have it," Mrs. Duncan said, placing the list on her desk. Leigh raised her hand. "And don't even ask if you can switch partners."

Leigh put her hand down.

"How will you know if we're really doing what we're supposed to?" asked Abigail Sundquist, a tall, friendly girl who was in Leigh's American Studies class.

"Each infant simulator has a tiny record bank. A computer chip will record when Baby cries and how long it took for you to soothe it. And each of you will wear a plastic wristband that contains a key that will stop Baby from crying." Mrs. Duncan grinned. "There's no easy way out here, folks. Everything's explained in the information packet. I want you to read through it for next time—it's very short."

Mrs. Duncan told them that they'd spend the next class learning more about parenting and this program and then would receive the dolls. She also reminded everyone that they were very expensive. If a student damaged one, not only would he or she fail that portion of the class, he or she would have to pay for any necessary repairs.

"This is going to be a great project!" Mrs. Duncan shouted over the noisy din of students gathering their things and bolting for the door at the sound of the bell. "You're going to enjoy it!"

"So what do you think?" Jason asked as the four of them walked down the hall.

"I think it's going to be fun," Leigh said. She loved to learn things that she could actually apply to real life. And what could be more real than this?

"I just hope you're a good mother, partner,"

Christian warned her teasingly.

"Are you kidding? I've only spent the past three years baby-sitting every kid within a two-block radius of my house. If I can't take care of a doll, I'm in serious trouble."

"This is a lot different than baby-sitting," Kerry said. "Taking that doll everywhere we go—to color guard practice? To the mall? Does she really think we're going to bring it to the movies and stuff?" She rolled her eyes. "I don't think so."

"It's only for four days, though," Jason pointed out. "That's nothing. Besides, girls love seeing guys all mushy and tender. Seeing me carry a doll around should pull in some positive female attention, don't you think?"

Kerry gave his cheek a pinch. "Sure, it will, sweetie-partner. That's why I definitely think *you* should be in charge of the doll all weekend long. I wouldn't want to jeopardize any possible love interests for you."

"What?" Jason threw his hand up to his throat in mock horror. "And deny my child his mother? You must be joking."

Leigh stopped walking. "I just remembered. I've got an eye exam scheduled for Friday morning that I need to tell the office about." Her mom had forgotten to call for an appointment until the middle of August, and by then the doctor had been booked solid for the rest of the summer.

"Okay. Call me later," Kerry said.

"See you in study hall," Christian told her.

Jason saluted as he broke off and headed toward the stairwell.

"Bye." Leigh watched as Christian slung his muscular arm around Kerry's shoulders and guided her through the throng.

Even though he dressed pretty much like all the other guys at Fillmore, there was something that set Christian apart. The way his jeans fit—loose, but just snug enough to show that he had a great body—his slightly oversized T-shirt, the casual way he carried his jacket over his shoulder . . .

Shaking her head, Leigh hurried off to the office.

She definitely needed to get her eyes checked again. Since when did she notice how a guy carried his jacket?

Yep, I am **READING.**
And Yep, this is a **Penguin.**

$0.50 US Only

TP4872-1 6/13 Printed in Guangdong, China
Fabriqué en Guangdong, Chine
Ages 6 and up   6 ans et plus

Scholastic Inc.
New York, NY
Scholastic Canada Ltd.
Markham Ontario
Scholastic Australia Pty. Ltd
Gosford NSW

341766

Four

I F YOU ASKED Leigh, last-period study hall had to be the invention of sadistic teachers who needed to get a life. Who else would insist on keeping students in school when they were through with classes for the day? In Leigh's school in California, people had been allowed to go home if their last period was a study hall. But not here in good old Fillmore. Here students were forced to watch the archaic metal clock tick slowly away, the second hand always stuttering on the 10 before making its final go-round.

Leigh let out a sigh Wednesday afternoon as she sucked on the ends of her hair and tried to concentrate. She'd been attempting to read the world's most boring chemistry passage for the past fifteen minutes, but each time she got to the part about how the 2 in $Ca(NO_3)_2$ stood for two nitrate radicals, she had to start over. The letters on the page stubbornly refused to make sense.

She was just on the verge of a mental meltdown when a small, neatly folded square of paper landed on her desk. Startled, Leigh looked up, but all she saw was a sea of heads staring down at desks.

The handwriting was loopy but neat.

> Tonight me, you, Kerry, & Jason at Jerry's, 7:30. I've got a major craving for suicide wings.
> C.

Leigh glanced across the room. Christian sat hunched over his desk, appearing to be deep in thought. Then he looked up from the book in front of him, folded his arms under his armpits, and flapped them back and forth like a bird.

Leigh giggled in spite of herself, then quickly checked to make sure that Mr. Simms, the study hall proctor, didn't notice. Leigh scrawled in purple ink underneath Christian's message:

> Sounds good, Chicken Dancer, but make mine mild! I'll meet you guys there.

She handed the note off to River Williams behind her, who surreptitiously slipped it through a chain of experienced note-passing hands to Christian.

He opened it, then gave Leigh a thumbs-up and one of his heart-twisting smiles.

A smile that could make a girl's heart skip a

frustrating beat. Leigh hunkered back down over her textbook.

A smile that could make finishing a chemistry passage all but impossible to do.

"This is one thing I definitely missed." Christian leaned back and licked hot sauce from his lips. "No one does wings like Jerry."

Leigh couldn't agree more. The black tables and cherry red booths, the TVs turned to local sports shows touting the Buffalo Bills, the buckets of aromatic wings that sat on the counter waiting for a waitress to deliver them to eager wing connoisseurs . . . Leigh had been there enough times over the past year that the restaurant was imprinted in her brain.

Jerry's was one of the best wing places in Buffalo. It didn't look like much from the outside: white aluminum siding, peeling red shingles, a neon sign that flashed Wings: Hot, Hotter, Suicide! But inside, the place was always packed. And the wings were awesome—tender, meaty, with a spicy addictive tang. Jerry's sauce ingredients were a well-kept secret. Other places tried to figure out just what made his recipe tick, but they never came close.

"You were probably too busy eating all that English stuff, like muffins and tea," Jason offered, munching on a piece of celery. His tall, six-foot frame was scrunched into the little vinyl booth next to Leigh.

Leigh swirled a carrot stick in the container of blue cheese dressing that was on their table. Not exactly the healthiest of meals, but once in a while was okay.

"Was the food really awful?" Kerry asked, stroking Christian's arm.

Christian grinned. "You haven't lived until you've eaten bangers and mash."

"I'm afraid to ask," Jason said.

"Sausages and mashed potatoes." Christian patted his stomach. "Yum. And the milk is extracreamy, plus they've got a lot of cereals and cookies and stuff that we don't have here." Then he wrinkled his nose. "But when it comes to salad dressing, they're hurting. They use this stuff called salad cream, and they only have, like, two different flavors. One of them looks and tastes like mayo."

"Eww!" Leigh and Kerry said in unison.

"Do they have pizza?" Jason asked. Leigh could tell by Jason's expression that he would never visit England if the answer was no.

"Sure. It's a lot more expensive there, though. Almost everything is." His expression turned pensive. "But it was worth every pence."

"Did you ever hear of a town called York?" Leigh asked. "My mother has relatives who live there."

"Really?" Christian's face lit up. "York is cool. There's this church called the York Minster that has amazing stained glass."

Kerry selected a wing from the greasy cardboard

bucket. "Saint Peter's has beautiful stained glass right here in Buffalo," she said, carefully dipping the meat into the extra suicide sauce they'd ordered. "What's the big deal?"

Christian shook his head. "I'm sure it's nice and everything, but it's not the same. In York you're standing in a place that's over four hundred years old! America doesn't have anything like that. There's this window there. . . ." Christian furrowed his brow. "Something to do with flowers." He shook his head. "Well, I don't remember what the name is, but if you look at it when the sun is behind it, the thing is totally incredible. The beauty is kind of overwhelming."

Jason tossed a bone onto a spare plate. "'The beauty is kind of overwhelming,'" he said in a high-pitched English accent. Kerry and Leigh dissolved into laughter. "I think you've been watching too much *Masterpiece Theater,* pal," he added.

Christian grinned good-naturedly. "Sounds crazy, but if you could see it . . ." He paused. "Guess you just had to be there."

"Did you ever make it to the moors?" Leigh asked, nibbling on a wing.

"The Moores? Are they relatives of yours?" Jason joked.

Leigh rolled her eyes. "No, dopey. The moors are this really wild part of England where the land-scape is all rocky and rural. Where *Wuthering Heights* takes place."

"Did it mention that in the Cliffs Notes?" Jason asked.

Christian finished his soda. "The moors were kind of far. The school took us on day trips to nearby places, like Oxford and Cambridge. And the Bonhams took me up to Scotland, and we stopped in York along the way. I heard the moors were cool, though."

Kerry took a sip of her Pepsi. "I'd like to see the United States. Go to Graceland, Mardi Gras in New Orleans, the Statue of Liberty, places like that."

Leigh nodded agreeably. When her friends began talking over the possibility of a combined junior-senior class trip to New York City in the spring, her mind drifted off. She was pretty sure that she knew what the window Christian spoke of a few minutes earlier looked like. She had a book called *The Great Churches of the World,* and the York Minster was included in it.

"Is, um, the window round, with lots of blue glass?" she ventured, breaking into the conversation.

"Huh?" Jason said.

"What are you talking about?" Kerry asked, crunching pieces of ice with her teeth.

Leigh blushed. She had this habit of thinking about things for a while before she spoke, then by the time she was ready to make a comment, everyone else was already two beats ahead of her. "The window in the church. I think it's called the Rose Window?"

"That's it!" Christian broke into a grin. "*Rose.* I should've remembered that—Mrs. Bonham had a whole garden of them in the backyard. I can't believe you've heard of it."

"I told you Leigh's into English stuff," Kerry reminded him. "You should've seen how she pored over the postcards you sent me."

"Only the fronts," Leigh added. Christian had sent Kerry cards from all the places Leigh hoped to visit one day—Piccadilly Circus, Trafalgar Square, Westminster Abbey. . . .

"You'll have to come over and see my pictures when I get them back," Christian told her. "I took about twenty rolls."

"I'd like that," Leigh replied.

As they waited for another order of wings to arrive, Jason and Kerry began to discuss the latest hot issue at Fillmore: If student council fund-raisers were used to support the boys' sports program, what about the girls' basketball team and the volleyball league?

Christian turned to Leigh. "I'm outta the loop on this one."

"Me too." Of course she thought that the girls' teams should get equal support, but she wasn't as into the whole debate thing as Kerry. England was infinitely more interesting.

"What were your classes like?" she asked Christian, tuning out Kerry's threat of a schoolwide student council protest.

"I took a really cool one called Art in London," Christian told her. "We studied sculpture and medieval art and British painting, and then we'd go see the real thing."

"That is so cool!"

Christian nodded. "Same with the theater—I took a drama class and we went to see six different plays, everything from experimental fringe shows to a big budget musical in the West End. It was great—I read *Macbeth* sophomore year, and I got to see the Royal Shakespeare Company perform it."

"I had a really tough time getting through that play. Seeing it live would help so much," Leigh said wistfully.

Christian poured Leigh a refill of her Pepsi. "Did you have World Culture Studies with Mr. Richmond last year?"

"You mean Sparky?" Legend had it that he'd been shocked so many times while plugging in his slide projector that his nerves were permanently damaged.

"They still call him that?" Christian laughed. "Poor guy'll never live that down."

"Is it really true?"

Christian scratched his head. "Have you ever seen hair like his on a normal person?"

Leigh giggled. "I did like his class. But experiencing world culture like you did sounds way better."

The two of them gabbed on and on. The pomp. The pageantry. The princes. The people.

The people. Leigh had been so absorbed in their conversation that she'd forgotten about Kerry and Jason, who were watching and listening to them with bemused expressions on their faces.

"Are you guys about through?" Jason yawned.

"All this stuff about the monarchy and painting can put a guy to sleep."

"Not that it's not interesting, but we do have more important things to discuss." Kerry clasped Christian's hands midcelery dip. "Like when are you going to talk to Coach Johnson about getting back on the Raiders?"

Jason bit into his tenth wing. "You were the team's star halfback, man. You were even better than the seniors."

Leigh knew Christian had been an awesome football player. But she couldn't picture him suited up in the Raiders' green-and-red uniforms. The guys on the football team were big and beefy. Loud. Hairy. Christian was sensitive. Thoughtful. Sweet. At least he seemed like he was. Leigh didn't know too many football players who were interested in stained glass—or who knew that the House of Windsor wasn't a place you could drop by for coffee.

"And you'd be varsity this year," Kerry added.

Christian looked uncomfortable. "I've kind of been thinking of sitting out this season."

"You mean not play?" Kerry sounded horrified.

"I want to devote more time to soccer."

"You play soccer?" Leigh asked. "I used to play when I was younger."

"Yeah. I started playing in England. I love it."

"Soccer's cool," Jason agreed. "But basketball is cooler."

Christian raised an eyebrow. "Easy for you to say." Jason's prowess on the court was legendary.

"But soccer's so . . . low profile," Kerry said disappointedly. "You're such a great football player. You could get a scholarship."

Christian shrugged. "I'll think about it."

"We had some awesome tailgate parties," Kerry reminded him. "Remember the time we set up the Crock-Pot of chili in the back of your parents' minivan, and it was so cold the chili froze?" She giggled. "And how about the time we stole the mascot uniform from Westcott High—you had to keep that furry polar bear outfit in your closet for a month!"

"That was crazy," Christian agreed, laughing.

As Kerry began to recount another funny story from the past, a part of Leigh longed to be able to do the same thing with her pals back in California. She knew how comforting it was to laugh over old jokes and cherished memories. But she also knew that you had to move on. No one could live in the past. And that was a good thing.

Because life in the present was much more interesting.

The moon hung heavily overhead as Christian and Kerry walked out to his dad's car. The temperature had dropped sharply from the warmth of the afternoon, and Christian shivered in his thin blue knit shirt. He was trying to avoid having to wear a jacket for as long as possible. Far too many months in Buffalo were spent wrapped in ski parkas and fleece caps. He wanted to hang on to the Indian summer as long as he could.

Christian opened Kerry's door for her, then walked around to his side.

"Still a gentleman," Kerry marveled, sliding into her seat.

"Some things never change," Christian quipped as he started the car and shifted into drive.

Kerry looked pretty tonight, her long blond hair pulled back in a twist, her eyelids dusted with a light sweep of pale green shadow. When he'd first laid eyes on her after all those months away, it had felt like coming home. The soft brush of her cheek against his, the sweet smell of her hair, the way her body curved up so naturally next to his.

During his last weeks in England he'd tried to imagine their reunion in his mind, but he never was quite able to do it. Even though he'd had her picture by his bedside, the Kerry in his mind had grown out of focus after a few months, and no matter how hard he'd tried, he began to lose the memory of what it felt like to be with her.

Kerry reached up and gave the little pine tree air freshener that hung from the rearview mirror a spin. "You know, I think this is the same one you had in here before you left."

"Probably is. My dad never replaces them."

"If you want, I can drive you to Target tomorrow to get a new one." Kerry's eyes twinkled.

Christian laughed as he pulled out into the street. "Man, that's right! I almost forgot—you got your license." He lowered his voice. "That is, if the DMV didn't change its mind."

Kerry swatted his arm. "I'll have you know that I've been driving for two months now. I'm a pro."

"Good thing. It's been so long since I drove that I might need your expertise." He'd thought the cars in England were some kind of joke when he'd first seen them—they were about half the size of the smallest American compacts. Riding in them in congested London traffic was kind of scary. Driving one was hair-raising. Not to mention the driving on the other side of the road business.

Kerry wrinkled her nose. "Didn't taking buses everywhere stink? I'd hate it."

"No, you wouldn't," Christian said. "The English public transportation system is really cool. I took the bus around Ealing, where I lived, and when Simon and I wanted to go into London, we'd just hop on the tube." Simon was Christian's host brother and one of his best English "mates." He was the same age as Christian, and they'd hit it off right away. He'd already called Christian twice since he'd returned.

"Don't teenagers there want to drive, though?"

"Yeah, but it's not that big a deal. And when it comes to drinking, the whole thing's reversed. There, you can be fourteen and go to your local pub and get a pint to drink. Here, that would never happen."

As they drove down Maple Avenue, Christian sighed inwardly. He'd been trying for days to describe his life in England to Kerry: the bustling London suburb of Ealing, filled with trendy shops and quaint pubs and great people; the thrill of seeing things like Big Ben and standing in the middle of Piccadilly Circus; the excitement of being on his own in a foreign country, forced to reach out to new people and learn new ways of living. But instead he ended up justifying public transportation.

Kerry popped a piece of gum into her mouth. "Well, anyway, doesn't it feel great to be home?" They pulled to a stop at a red light. "I know you must've been dying to go to Jerry's. And for some of your mom's great cooking."

Christian nodded. "That alone was worth the price of my airfare."

Kerry ran her fingernail along the edge of the seat belt. "And seeing me."

"And seeing you."

Kerry and Christian, together again. People had been coming up to them in the hall, "congratulating" him at his locker, happy at their resumed couple status. *You guys were meant to be together. You make such a cute couple! Long-distance love really does work.*

To be honest, though, getting back together wasn't turning out to be quite that easy. Christian couldn't believe he was feeling this way, but it was kind of weird to be with Kerry again. He hadn't expected this. They'd been E-mailing each other all year, and he'd sent her funny postcards every few weeks while she'd sent him long letters complete with detailed cartoons. They'd been so close when he left. . . .

But he'd returned somebody else. He'd devel-

45

oped new interests, experienced another culture. And things were definitely different.

Just then Kerry put her hand on his shoulder. "Earth to Christian."

He flushed. "Sorry. Just spacing out a little, I guess. Every now and then I can't believe I'm here."

Kerry slid her hand down and squeezed his bicep. "Well, you are. And I'm so . . . I—" She paused. "I just missed you so much," she said finally.

"I missed you too." Christian met her gaze and smiled. There were times in England that he couldn't wait to see Kerry, to tell her about everything that had happened to him while he was away. To share a funny joke or amaze her with the latest goofball thing one of his new friends did.

And now he was here, back in Buffalo, and he had all the time in the world to talk to her.

If he could just stop feeling so awkward.

Christian concentrated on the road instead, guiding the car down the dark, leaf-littered streets and into Kerry's half-circular driveway. The Coles' Dutch Colonial greeted him like a stately old friend, so different from the tidy, stone-faced houses with brightly painted doors and small, postage-stamp-size lawns his neighborhood in South Ealing had.

Kerry popped open her seat belt and went for the door handle. "You are coming in, aren't you?" she asked.

Christian hesitated. He'd planned on hanging out for a while, but suddenly he was feeling tired.

Yet when he saw the disappointment registering in Kerry's face, he killed the ignition. "Sure."

They walked up the sidewalk hand in hand, Kerry's heels clicking against the smooth stone surface. Christian had forgotten how her hand felt in his, how they used to lace their fingers together. Without quite knowing why, he squeezed Kerry's hand lightly. She squeezed back and took out her fuzzy bear key ring, holding it up under the moonlight.

"That darn old house key," Christian said softly as they reached the front porch. He wondered if she'd remember the game. They'd played it whenever Christian walked her to the door: Kerry would pretend she couldn't find the key, and Christian would take advantage of the time outside to kiss her.

"Funny, isn't it? I only have trouble with it when you're here," she remarked. She bent her head, going along with him as Christian leaned forward and—

Suddenly the front porch light snapped on and the door opened.

"Christian!" Mrs. Cole cupped Christian's startled face and planted a kiss on his cheek. "We're so glad you're back with us!"

"Thanks, Mrs. C." Kerry's mom was an older, heavier, and just as much fun version of Kerry, with highlighted blond hair and an infectious laugh.

Embarrassed, Kerry ducked under her mom's arms and shook off her jacket. "Mom, didn't you maul him enough the other night?"

Mrs. Cole gave his hair a loving rumple. "We missed your smile around this place."

Kerry swept by her. "I'm so thirsty," she declared, striding into the kitchen and pouring herself a glass of water.

Christian followed, his eyes taking in all the details. Ever since he'd returned, entering the Coles' house was like walking back in time. He'd forgotten how well he knew every part of it: the smooth, honeyed molding of the stairway railing, the polished oak floors, the way the light spilled out cozily from the country-style kitchen. Heck, he *should* know every detail—he'd spent practically every other night here a year ago, eating supper with the Coles, working on homework, rooting for the Bills with Kerry and her family. He'd felt almost as at home here as he did at his own house.

"I just put the teakettle on for Dad and me," Mrs. Cole said. "Can I get you anything, Christian?"

"Save me some water—I might have some tea," Christian replied.

Kerry shot him a surprised look. "Tea? Since when?"

"Um . . . since my first week in England, I guess." The Bonhams had tea for breakfast, tea for an afternoon snack, and tea at night. Becoming a tea drinker hadn't been a choice—it was a mandate.

"We're going to go watch TV downstairs," Kerry told her mom. "Make sure the freak stays

48

away from us."

Mrs. Cole frowned. "Despite what you might think, *Timmy* is just as entitled to roam these halls as you are. But don't worry." Mrs. Cole looked fondly at Christian. "Not that we don't love to have you here, Christian, but I'm afraid you can't stay too long. It's almost nine-thirty, and Kerry needs to spend some more time on her homework tonight."

"Mom, I already did my French and my math problems," Kerry protested.

"Great. But I didn't realize that those were your only classes," Mrs. Cole said dryly.

Kerry rolled her eyes.

"I'll leave by ten," Christian promised, ushering Kerry down the hall. He needed to go home and start going through the college catalogs that had built up over the summer. He'd never given much thought to college, assuming he'd go somewhere local like UB or Buffalo State. But now he wasn't so sure. Maybe he'd apply to NYU—he could major in art history. Or theater.

"She's really on my case this year about studying," Kerry griped.

"Yeah, well, junior year's pretty important, Ker. Those A's you'll be pulling in precalc will help determine where you go to college."

"Since when did you become such a bookworm?"

Christian wrinkled his nose at that categorization. He'd never made the honor roll or anything, but this year he intended to get serious. "Just trying to use my senior expertise to help you, that's all."

Kerry plopped down on one of the oversized stuffed chairs in the gigantic family room and patted the spot next to her. "You can help me right here, señor." Obediently Christian wedged in beside her. It was a tight squeeze.

"You really have grown," Kerry said, shaking her head in amusement.

"Yeah, my mom said the same thing when we were at the Gap the other night." Christian stretched out his legs on the ottoman in front of them as Kerry turned on the TV and started flipping through the channels.

Seinfeld reruns, *Dateline, I Love Lucy* on Nickelodeon—the shows blipped by. "I heard that there are only, like, four channels in Europe or something," Kerry said. "I'd die before I'd give up cable."

"You've got fifty channels here, but is there really anything you want to watch?"

"Nope." Kerry tossed the remote aside and snuggled into him. "All I want to watch is you."

Instinctively Christian lifted his head, and Kerry tucked hers under his chin. They used to sit that way all the time. It was funny how he'd forgotten about it until now.

Christian tried to focus on the TV—some program about animal activists freeing grocery store lobsters in Maine—but he couldn't. All he could do was think. He'd been doing a lot of that lately.

Does she want me to kiss her? He wasn't sure. Playing it safe, he pretended to yawn. As he stretched back he put his arm around Kerry, his hand resting lightly on her shoulder.

An unexpected wave of uneasiness washed over him. *What is wrong with me?* he berated himself, shifting in the chair. Kerry shifted too, positioning herself even closer. *There's nothing to be nervous about. It's just Kerry.*

Trying not to be obvious, Christian wiped a slightly sweaty palm on his leg. Should he tell her how he was feeling? But what would he say? That he'd felt, well, just a little funny about things since he got back? He couldn't. The words would come out all wrong. It wasn't that Christian didn't want to be here with her, because he did. He wasn't the type of guy to do things he didn't want to do or be with people he didn't want to be with.

He shifted again.

"Are you comfortable?" Kerry asked, turning her big green eyes to look questioningly at him. "We could sit on the couch together if you want. There's more room."

"No, this is fine, Ker."

"Do you want me to go get you that cup of tea?"

Christian nodded. "Thanks. With a splash of milk."

Kerry hoisted herself up. "Your wish is my command." She leaned over and kissed him lightly on the lips. "Be right back."

"Okay." Christian settled back in the chair, trying to act casual. Kerry's parents were upstairs, and here they were alone in the family room, the lights low, the TV playing some show neither one of them cared

51

about. You didn't have to be a genius to figure out what was going to happen in the next few minutes.

Christian took a deep breath. You also didn't have to be a genius to know that you shouldn't be making out with someone if you weren't really, really into her. And suddenly, frighteningly, he wasn't sure if he was.

Was he crazy? Why was he feeling this way all of a sudden? Kerry hadn't changed. She was the same peppy, bubbly girlfriend he'd said good-bye to last year. Sure, her hair was a little longer, her curves a little more developed, her laugh a little throatier. But she was his girlfriend.

Girlfriend.

His. And he loved being with her. *So what is my problem?* Christian thought, his mind a jumble of mismatched thoughts. Each time he saw her, Christian found himself growing more uneasy rather than more comfortable. Did she feel it too? He didn't know. But he did know that Kerry expected him to act like he used to. And why wouldn't she?

Being a boyfriend wasn't hard. All he had to do was put his arm around her, hold her tight, kiss her, and tell her that things were going to be great between them, that he'd missed her so much.

And it's true, a voice inside his head told him.

But for some unexplainable reason he couldn't do that. He just couldn't seem to make himself act like a boyfriend.

I just need some time, Christian decided. *Give it some time. It'll all work out. Quit worrying.*

"Here you go." Kerry came back down the stairs, handed him a steaming mug of tea, and sat back down beside him.

"Thanks." Christian took a tentative sip, the strong smell of orange pekoe warming his nostrils, and placed the mug gently down on the end table. Maybe it would be better if he talked to Kerry about what was bugging him. Maybe she was feeling the same way. That had been what was so great about their relationship. They were so open with each other, so comfortable.

"Kerry?"

"Hmmm?" She cuddled in closer.

Christian hesitated. Were things really that different, or was he only imagining them to be? After all, he'd only been back for less than a week. There was no way anyone could expect them to leap back into their relationship after being apart for a whole year, right?

"It's good to see you again," he blurted out. And as he looked into those green eyes he knew so well, the doubts he'd had a moment before sifted through his veins like finely grained sand.

Kerry stared over at him, then laughed. "Likewise."

Christian smiled sheepishly, then pulled Kerry close, nestling her in the crook of his arm.

He was just being paranoid, that was all. All they needed was a little more time. So what if they weren't the same two people they were when he'd left? In a few weeks they'd be back where they'd left off.

Right?

Five

"CHECK OUT THIS new crochet dress. I've *got* to get this."

Leigh turned to look at Rochelle, her gossipy, heavily made-up coworker at the Sweater Set. Rochelle was supposed to be making sure that the right sizes were in the right places—brown sweaters in piles of small, medium, and large. But instead she was staring longingly at a new window display someone had hung that afternoon.

"Isn't it nice?" Rochelle said, touching the material.

Leigh raised her eyebrows. "Are you sure it's a dress? I thought it was a vest."

Rochelle's big eyes lingered thoughtfully on Leigh. "You'd look terrific in it," she declared.

"Really?" Leigh stared at the vest, rather, dress.

Rochelle sighed as she went to unlock a dressing

54

room for a customer. "If I had a body like yours, you'd better believe I'd wear it."

Leigh glanced at her reflection in the mirror. She was no Pamela Lee, but she had begun to "fill out," as her mom would say. Last year she'd grown an inch, and gone were the discouraging days when she could skip wearing a bra and no one would notice.

Leigh returned to the table of sweaters she'd been working on. Side, side. Arm, arm. Fold once. Check the size. Place on shelf. Leigh deftly folded one knit top after the next. A thankless task, really, because as soon as she had one stack of clothing organized, some customer would come along, hold a sweater at arm's length, and after a few seconds carelessly discard it back on the table.

The Sweater Set was one of the more popular stores in the mall, selling everything from pastel-colored twinsets to fleecy zip-up polos. Leigh usually worked one weekend shift and one school night. She liked having the extra money, even though she ended up giving most of it back to the store itself. Who could pass up a forty-percent discount?

She was just bending down to pick up a shirt that had fallen out of one of the store's cubicles when a familiar voice chirped, "Hi! Do you sell sweaters?"

Leigh lifted her head to see Kerry standing with Christian, toting a shopping bag from Nine West. She wore a fuzzy pale green shirt that accentuated her eyes and formfitting olive suede pants. Christian looked like he'd just disembarked from a fishing trawler with his flushed red cheeks, knit cap, and woolly black fisherman's sweater.

Except most fishermen didn't have a Snugli carrier around their neck or a bright red diaper bag slung over their shoulders.

"Hey," Christian said, smiling. His hazel eyes glittered in the harsh overhead track lights.

"Hi, guys!" Leigh stood up, her stomach unexplainably lurching. "What's up?"

Kerry yawned. "Doing the parent thing."

"Say hi to Charlie," Christian said, jostling the Snugli.

Mrs. Duncan had passed out the dolls in class on Thursday, and when Christian had declared theirs looked like a Charlie, Leigh hadn't argued. She reached over to tweak the doll's toe, her arm brushing lightly against Christian's stomach. The touch sent a sliver of electricity up her spine, causing her cheeks to flush with embarrassment. What was wrong with her?

Leigh fidgeted with her spoon necklace. "Has he been behaving?" she asked.

"It's a losing battle," Kerry said, looking at Christian and shaking her head with mock disgust.

Christian wiggled his eyebrows. "The kid's an angel. Takes after his old man."

Leigh laughed.

"We just grabbed a bite over at the food court, and everyone was looking at us," Kerry huffed. "At first they had these 'I can't believe those two *children* have a baby' expressions on their faces. And then, when they

56

realized it's a doll, they thought we were wacked."

"A few people asked what we were doing. They thought it was cool when we told them," Christian added. He dangled the care key from his wristband. "So far he's only cried once tonight, and that was because I laid him on his stomach when I was trying to unstrap the car seat."

"Very by the book," Leigh said, nodding. If they took the dolls in the car, they were supposed to use the car seats Mrs. Duncan had on loan from local baby stores.

"I hope Jason's doing a good job with Hyper," Kerry said. Jason and Kerry's doll had started crying the moment they got him. The name Hyper fit. "Somehow Jason doesn't seem the dad type."

"What makes you say that?" Leigh asked.

"Oh, only that he left Hyper in his locker yesterday morning for twenty minutes." Kerry sighed heavily. "We're going to be seriously penalized for that one."

"Where are you guys off to?"

"The movies," Kerry said.

"And a pit stop at that Mexican place." Christian patted his stomach. "The greasy beef taco special is awesome."

"Didn't you just eat?" Leigh asked.

Christian grinned. "Ready for round two."

Leigh grimaced. "I always wondered who actually ate at Château Taco."

The dimple in Christian's cheek deepened. "Just poor slobs like me."

For a moment Leigh remembered the night she'd first seen Christian. *That smile, those eyes, that hair . . .*

Your best friend's boyfriend . . . Leigh blinked back to reality and began to systematically straighten a teetering stack of chenille sweaters. "What are you going to see?" she asked, her eyes focused on the industrial beige carpet beneath her.

"That alien movie, about the killer earthworms?" Christian covered Charlie's ears. "Don't want to scare the little fellow."

"The one where the earthworms multiply from Earth's core and start invading people's lawns?" Leigh burst out. "I'm dying to see it!"

"But you hate sci-fi flicks!" Kerry said. "You covered your eyes all through *Alien Flame*!"

"Yeah, but how can I make fun of them if I don't see them?"

"Good point." Christian turned to Kerry. "We could walk around until Leigh gets out of work and then all go to the movies together."

Kerry cleared her throat. "Leigh works until ten, though," she pointed out.

Leigh got the odd sensation that she'd sabotaged things somehow—some crucial couple moment between Christian and Kerry. *Kerry doesn't want me to go,* Leigh realized. *She wants to be alone with Christian.* And with the weird vibes she was feeling tonight, she was definitely better off going home alone to *Letterman*. "Uh, yeah," Leigh backtracked, nodding. "Kerry's right. Thanks, though."

The muscles in Kerry's jaw relaxed. "If you could get out early or something . . ."

"I don't mind missing the first few minutes of the movie," Christian assured her. "All they do is show ten minutes of trailers anyway."

"I really shouldn't." Leigh faked a big, tonsily yawn. "I'm feeling kind of tired. Folding sweaters will do that to you."

Kerry shrugged. "Well, if you're sure . . . ?"

Leigh nodded. "Yep. You guys can tell me all about it."

"The earthworm dudes are gonna miss you," Christian told her as Kerry crooked her arm in his. "Now's your last chance."

Leigh laughed, shooing them out. "Be good to Charlie."

Kerry shot her an appreciative glance as she and Christian exited the store.

"Who was that?" Rochelle hurried over, adjusting her name tag. "He was so cute!"

"My friend's boyfriend." Leigh lifted her hair off her perspiring neck. Why was it so hot in here suddenly?

"Really? By the way he was looking at you, I'd say he was with the wrong girl."

"What?" Leigh felt her nerves go limp. That was the craziest thing she'd heard all day. All week, for that matter. "You don't know what you're talking about."

Rochelle shrugged and began to organize a rack of sweater vests, whistling the theme from *The*

Nanny. Every few seconds she glanced at Leigh.

"Go on, get it off your chest," Leigh said finally, knowing that if she didn't tell Rochelle to speak up, she'd spend the rest of the night feeling her coworker's eyes on her.

"It just seemed like there was something between you two—some chemistry."

"Chemistry?"

Rochelle nodded. "You know, lingering glances, nervous smiles, lots of blushing."

"The only chemistry I know anything about these days involves nitrates and phosphates." A line had now formed at the cash registers at the back of the store, and Leigh hurried back to wait on the next customer.

Rochelle's ridiculous, Leigh thought. If she had any reaction to Christian at all, it had to be the cute guy thing. Whether it was Christian or a total stranger, talking to a hot guy always threw her.

"About time you got here," seethed Nadine, a tall, prim-nosed college student who'd worked at the store one week longer than Leigh had and acted as if she'd been an employee since birth. "I've been *extremely* busy."

"It's called work," Leigh muttered under her breath. She snatched up a scanner and began ringing up the next customer's purchase. A woolly black fisherman's sweater.

"We have some terrific knit caps that look really cute with these. . . ."

★   ★   ★

Leigh could hardly wait to get home and kick off the black leather boots she'd worn to work. Folding sweaters and smiling at customers was easy, but standing on her feet for five hours straight, three of them next to Nadine, was painful. Her mom had surprised her by saving her a plate of her delicious fettuccine Alfredo—she'd even sprinkled fresh mozzarella on top and baked it until the cheese got brown and bubbly, just how Leigh liked it.

After she ate, Leigh and her mom put on their pajamas and watched the eleven o'clock news and then *Letterman*. But before Dave had finished his monologue, Leigh's eyes fought a losing battle to stay open. She kissed her mom good night and stumbled down the hallway to her room. Telling Kerry and Christian she'd been tired wasn't a lie after all.

She'd just fallen into the first few moments of a deep sleep when the shrill ring of the telephone on her nightstand startled her.

"Hello?" Leigh mumbled, picking up.

"Hey, it's me." Kerry's voice was low. "Did I wake you?"

"No," Leigh whispered, fumbling for the clock. It was twelve-thirty.

"Tell your parents I'm really, really sorry I'm calling so late."

Leigh pulled her pillow under her head, propping herself up. "They're such sound sleepers that Prodigy could be in our living room and they'd never know. What's wrong?"

"Can't sleep . . . I'm feeling restless," Kerry said. "Edgy."

"Why?"

Big sigh. "Tonight was so . . . so disappointing."

"Did you and Christian have a fight?" Leigh asked.

"No, but at least that would have been interesting."

Leigh hesitated. "What do you mean?"

"Well, we got something to eat and came and saw you, walked around the mall, went to the movies, and then went home."

"Right . . . *and?*" Leigh prompted.

"Two people who haven't seen each other in a year, and we had nothing intelligent to say to each other."

"You guys did seem a little off," Leigh confided, rolling onto her side.

"We did? Like how?"

"I don't know; nothing hugely weird. Just a little tense, maybe. Kind of anxious."

Kerry sighed again. "This is a totally bad way to start."

Leigh took off the ankle socks she'd worn to bed and tossed them on the floor. "Maybe you're making a bigger deal out of tonight than you should. How was the movie?"

"Okay. But sitting quietly in the theater for two hours didn't do much to advance our relationship either."

"You were together the whole night—you must have talked some."

"Yeah, but it's like we're on two different wave-lengths. Christian talks a lot about England and his friends there and stuff, and I try to be interested. And I am, somewhat, but I'm more interested in talking about us, about the stuff we like to do."

"Like what?"

"I don't know—football games, listening to music, watching TV, hanging out." Kerry paused. "Basic things, really, but I never thought they were basic when we were together. We made them fun."

Leigh thought back to the conversation Wednesday night at Jerry's. "You guys have changed, though."

"I haven't!" Kerry burst out.

"Were you on color guard when Christian left?"

"No . . ."

"How about student council?"

"No, but—"

"And aren't you thinking about going out for track team this spring?"

"None of those things change me as a person!" Kerry protested.

"Sure, they do," Leigh argued. "And Christian's changed too. He plays soccer now instead of football. And just the other day you said he's gotten a lot more serious about school."

"But I don't think joining clubs and stuff is the issue," Kerry said with a sniffle. "It's more us as a couple that's worrying me."

Leigh thought for a moment. "Maybe instead of trying to do the kind of things you used to do, you should try to do something new together."

"Like what?"

"Anything. It seems to me that the more you try to capture what you had over a year ago, the harder it's going to be for you both to be happy."

"I don't know. Maybe." Kerry yawned. "I think I'm ready to sleep now."

"Was I that boring?"

"No, you were great. I just can't think about this anymore tonight."

"Well, I hope I helped."

"You did. Call me tomorrow."

"Okay. Bye."

"Bye."

Leigh clicked off and buried herself under the twisted covers, her mind spinning. There was so much to think about when you were in a relationship, so many problems that could come up. You really had to make sure that you were with the right person. If you were, working through everything would definitely be worth it. But if you weren't, it would be a waste of time—and of emotion.

Leigh hoped that for Kerry's sake, she would discover which situation she was in before it was too late.

Six

"HAND ME THE scissors, honey, will you?"
Leigh reached up and gave them to
her mom, who was perched on top of a wooden
stepladder in the Feralanos' bathroom. "It's starting
to look good in here." Today was a lazy, rainy
Saturday, and Leigh had offered to help her mom
around the house while her dad spent the afternoon
doing research in the study.

"Thanks." Leigh's mother smiled proudly. "That
design class gave me the extra spurt of motivation I
needed to get into gear this weekend." She carefully
trimmed a minuscule piece off the flowered pastel
border that now accented the room, then shot a
critical eye at the wall opposite the vanity. "Now all
I need to do is hang up that wicker shelf unit and
retile the floor in here and we'll be all set."

Leigh smiled. Knowing her mother, they'd be
redecorating for the next five years. When they'd

first bought the house, Mrs. Feralano had declared the place was in "move-in condition." Then she'd proceeded to promptly reface the kitchen cabinets, pull up the carpet in the living room, refinish the hardwood floor, and paint all three of the bedrooms. The master bath was her next pet project.

"Help me measure the distance here," Mrs. Feralano instructed.

Obligingly Leigh picked up the pencil that lay by the sink and helped her mother measure the space they had to work with.

"So how's school going, honey? Your teachers okay this year?"

"They're fine." Leigh made a little *x* with her pencil where one of the nails was to go.

Mrs. Feralano watched as Leigh made another *x*, then stepped back to judge their handiwork, her pencil in her mouth. "Haven't seen much of Kerry this week," she said through clenched teeth.

Leigh shrugged. "Well, you know. Christian's back, and she's kind of taken up with him." The soft pitter-patter of rain on the bathroom skylight grew more intense. It was really coming down hard now.

Mrs. Feralano tapped a tiny nail into one of the *x*'s. "They started right up where they left off, huh? Seems like it'd be kind of hard to do."

"Why do you say that?" Leigh asked.

Mrs. Feralano tapped in another nail. "They were a lot younger when they first started dating, weren't they? A year is quite a long time to be apart."

"But Kerry couldn't wait for him to come back. She missed him so much."

"I'm not saying she didn't miss him. But she might not feel the same way. And he might have changed too." Her mother picked up the wicker shelf. "How's that baby program going—didn't you say that you and Christian are partners?"

Leigh leaned against the doorway. "So far, so good. Christian had to keep the doll Thursday and Friday, and today he's supposed to come over and give it to me. We each get to keep it for two nights."

Mrs. Feralano nodded approvingly. "Sounds like an excellent class. Young people need to be aware that having a baby isn't at all compatible with a teenager's lifestyle."

Leigh didn't think she needed to carry a doll around all weekend to grasp that obvious point, but she supposed her mom was right. She helped her fold up the stepladder. "Feel like some hot chocolate?" Leigh asked.

"Sure, honey. Let me just get this stuff cleaned up."

Leigh went into the kitchen and took out a saucepan. She liked to make hot chocolate the old-fashioned way, with cocoa powder and milk, making sure to peel off the "skin" that formed on top when the milk began to boil. Just as she was leveling off the powder, the doorbell rang, the unexpected noise making her drop the cocoa tin on the counter. "I'll get it!" Leigh yelled. She righted the tin, wiped her hands on her sweatpants, and hurried to the door.

Christian stood on the step under the porch awning, attempting to shelter himself from the heavy downpour. He was cradling Charlie in his arms and holding an infant carrier. "Special delivery!"

"Hi!" Leigh motioned for him to come in out of the rain. "You're soaking wet!"

Christian held out a mangled mess of nylon, spokes, and metal. "This is what's left of my three-dollar umbrella." He grinned. "But I managed to keep little Charlie safe and dry under my shirt." He pulled the soggy navy polo away from his body.

"Let me get you a towel or something," Leigh said, tossing the ruined umbrella in the stand by the front door. "That's some rain out there, huh?"

"It's going to clear up soon. The sun's been trying to come out all day."

Leigh gestured to the kitchen. "Wait in there. I'll be right back."

She hurried down the hall, pulled a fluffy towel from the linen closet, and returned to the kitchen. Christian had seated himself on one of the bar stools at their kitchen island. His wet shirt was draped over another bar stool, leaving him clad only in his jeans and white cotton undershirt.

A damp white cotton undershirt.

A damp white, kind of clingy cotton undershirt.

"Here," she said, handing the towel to him in what she hoped was a casual manner.

"Thanks."

Leigh couldn't help watching Christian as he dried off his face and hair. The water had made his dark waves develop ringlets, and his cheeks were flushed a soft, rosy pink. He'd hung up his yellow windbreaker on the coat tree, and his boots were drying on the kitchen welcome mat. Charlie lay wrapped in a blanket in his infant carrier.

"I was just making some hot chocolate for my mom and me. Would you like to join us?" Leigh asked, suddenly shy at seeing Christian in her kitchen.

"That would be great."

Just then Leigh's mom walked into the room. "Mom, this is Christian. Christian, my mom," Leigh said.

"Hi, Mrs. Feralano. Nice to meet you. Sorry about the water."

"No problem." She gestured to the scissors, tape, wallpaper roll, glue, and hammer in her hands. "I'd shake your hand, but mine are a little full right now."

Christian grinned. "Next time."

"Is this my grandchild?" Mrs. Feralano asked, peering down at the doll. "I can see the family resemblance."

"Mom!" Leigh hated when her mother acted goofy.

But Christian laughed. He held up his arm, revealing the wristband. "I'd definitely let you babysit, but Mrs. Duncan has other ideas."

Mrs. Feralano gave a dramatic sigh. "Another time, then." She started out of the room. "Why don't you give Christian my cup of hot chocolate?" she called over her shoulder. "I want to go put these things away, and then I've got to make some phone calls."

"Your mom seems cool," Christian said, giving his head one last brisk rub with the towel. A hunk of dark hair stood straight up.

Fighting back the urge to fix it, Leigh busied herself by pouring milk into the saucepan. "She's okay." She took out two mugs out from the cupboard. "How's Charlie been?"

Christian stretched back his arms. "Not too bad. But last night he started crying about three in the morning, and I had to hold the key in place for almost thirty minutes," he told her. "I was practically falling asleep. And then, just when I thought I was home free, he started crying again at six this morning."

Leigh gave the milk a stir, then sat down beside him. "You must be so tired."

"A little." He took a deep breath. "Smells delicious."

"Thanks."

She noticed Christian staring at her neck, and she moved her hand to her throat self-consciously.

Christian blushed. "Sorry. I was just looking at that ring you wear around your neck. I noticed it the night Kerry threw me the party . . . when we danced."

"I always wear it," Leigh said, sliding the ring on her finger and off again.

"Is it from an old boyfriend?"

"No!" Leigh giggled. "From my grandma. It was a spoon from her teaspoon collection, and she had it made into a ring for me."

70

"It's nice."

"Thanks."

"I have an old pocket watch my grandpa gave me. He fought in the Korean War, and a guy he met while he was stationed there gave it to him. I keep it in a box underneath my T-shirts."

"Is your grandfather still alive?" Leigh asked, the pain of her grandmother's death still fresh to her.

"Yeah—he and Grandma Doris live on a golf course in Tampa. But I don't get to see them much." Christian began to tell her about his last visit there: His little sister had talked his grandparents into riding a superscary roller coaster at Busch Gardens. Afterward they'd walked around nursing headaches but proudly sporting I Survived a Brush with Death T-shirts.

Leigh couldn't stop laughing at the mental picture. And for the first time in her life Leigh felt comfortable—really comfortable—talking casually with a guy. Just as she was about to ask if he wanted another cup of cocoa, Christian looked up at the kitchen clock.

"Darn! I'm late."

"For what?"

Christian picked up his shoes and began to lace them up. "I told Kerry I'd be at her house by two o'clock; Jason's dropping Hyper off at six. We'd planned on renting a movie, but now that it's clearing up outside, I'd like to go for a bike ride."

"Oh. That sounds like fun. Biking's fun."

Leigh swallowed the rest of her hot chocolate.

"I live for it," Christian told her. "September's the best time to go—not too hot, not too cold. And the leaves are brilliant."

Leigh placed the mugs in the sink and put away the bottle of cinnamon and the bag of marshmallows. For some peculiar reason, her hands were shaking. What was her problem? It was just Christian.

"Thanks for bringing Charlie over," she said.

"We must be a good team. He hasn't made a sound the whole time I've been here," Christian remarked, giving the doll a little pat on the head. He shrugged into his windbreaker as they walked down the hallway to the front door. "Thanks again for the hot chocolate. Call me later if you need anything or if the doll is giving you problems, okay?"

"Okay." Leigh gave Christian a shy smile. "I'm glad you stopped by."

Christian moved forward slightly, his right arm reaching out. *Is he going to hug me?* Leigh thought suddenly, her back stiffening. But then he moved back and touched her gently on her forearm. "Bye."

"Bye."

Leigh's eyes followed Christian as he jogged back to his car, splashing through the puddles that had formed in the driveway. He hopped inside and pulled out into the street, making the familiar left turn toward Kerry's house.

As Leigh looked up at the sky she saw that a rainbow had blossomed—its reds, blues, and yellows touching down just past the grove of trees on the next block over.

Somewhere there was a pot of gold waiting to be discovered.

And somewhere there's a guy for me.

"Isn't it beautiful out?" Christian breathed in the crisp autumn air. He and Kerry had been cycling for almost three hours, and he still couldn't get enough. He leaned forward as they coasted down a small hill, the breeze whipping through his hair, the sun overhead drying off any lingering wet spots on his clothes.

They turned to the left in unison, pedaling down a long, curving street that was a favorite with bicyclists and joggers for several reasons: little traffic, a flat road, and gorgeous homes that lined the route.

"I haven't been over here in so long," Kerry said. "I forgot how nice it is."

"It's the best," he agreed as his tire rode over an acorn. His last summer here he and Kerry had gone biking almost every other day. They'd biked through each other's neighborhoods, down the trails that surrounded the park near Kerry's house—virtually anywhere their bikes would take them.

"Race you to the bridge!" Christian exclaimed suddenly. He sped ahead.

"No fair!" Kerry cried, her feet pumping furiously on her pedals.

Christian sped forward, the houses only a blur in his peripheral vision. To an outsider, the road looked like a dead end. But if you made a sharp right at the end, you'd see a narrow, dusty trail that lasted for several yards, ending at a small wooden bridge. Its span was only big enough to hold three bicycles from end to end, and its location ensured privacy for anyone who was able to find it.

Without looking behind him, Christian reached the path, turned for the bridge, and came to an abrupt stop at its entrance. Dust spewed up in little clouds.

Kerry was only a few feet behind. "Cheater!" she said, gasping for breath as she came up beside him. Wisps of blond hair clung to her flushed face. "I could've beat you if you'd given me fair warning!"

Christian hopped off his bike and leaned it against the bridge as Kerry followed suit. Impulsively he moved toward her. "Do you need fair warning for this?" he asked, then kissed her softly on the lips. The bridge had been their "spot" the summer before last—a place for rest stops and water breaks . . . as well as stolen kisses.

Kerry's lips were warm and tasted slightly of salt. After a few seconds Christian pulled away.

"Nope, no warning necessary," Kerry said lightly, hopping up on the bridge's railing. "Feel free to do it anytime."

Christian laughed, but inside, his stomach was churning. Kissing was like taking a lie detector test. After you kissed someone, you couldn't get away with thinking, *Maybe I love her, maybe I don't, I just don't know.* A kiss left little room for doubts. He'd almost been fooled into thinking that Kerry was the reason his spirits were so high. Not that she wasn't good company—she always was. But it was the act of biking itself—the great weather, the gorgeous foliage, coasting down a hill with your hands in the air and feeling on top of the world—that had made him feel so great today.

And one other thing. Something simple.

Hot chocolate. Warm and cocoa-y, with a hint of cinnamon spice and just enough whipped cream, accompanied by a smile that drove his heart to his knees.

"Just one more coat," Leigh said to herself. She dipped the brush into the new bottle of L'Oréal polish she'd picked up at the mall and expertly polished her right toe. She liked to do her nails on Sunday nights and prep for the week ahead.

"Braghhhhh!"

With a sigh Leigh tightly capped the bottle. Charlie had been crying off and on for hours. She'd spent most of last night taking care of him, and when he finally settled down, she couldn't fall back to sleep herself.

Charlie was lying on his back on her bed, surrounded by pillows and stuffed animals. She picked him up, making sure to hold him correctly. When he didn't stop crying, she fumbled to insert the care key in his back.

"There, there," she said, using the same technique she'd finally perfected last night. Leigh rocked Charlie back and forth.

"Leigh, the baby!" her mom called from the basement just as the crying stopped.

"I know!" Leigh yelled back, gripping the care key. She began to pace the room. Then she glanced down at her toes. Pale blue carpet fuzz stuck to her freshly polished nails.

The key slipped out.

"Braghhhh!"

"Do you need any help?" her dad called.

"No!" She reinserted the key and dropped down on her bed. Then she stood up. Then she took a deep breath. *Don't get rattled.*

Leigh racked her brain, trying to remember what Mrs. Duncan had told them. Was it normal for the doll to need care for over ten minutes? She checked her alarm clock. Well, only three silent minutes had passed. But it felt like twenty. Leigh knew she was supposed to wait for the doll to start crying again before she removed the key, but he'd been quiet for a while. Maybe she could just try taking the key out and—

"Braghhhh!"

Leigh put the key back in, silencing the doll. Sure, he'd cried a lot last night, but each time he'd stopped and started up again within a few seconds of inserting the key.

After fifteen legitimate minutes had passed and Charlie was still quiet, Leigh started to panic. What if the electronic box recorded neglect? What if she was responsible for her and Christian failing this part of the course?

Ringgg!

Charlie? Or the phone?

Phone.

"Hello?" Leigh cried, by now completely frazzled.

"Leigh?"

"Yes?"

"It's Christian."

"Thank God!" Before Christian could say a word, Leigh hurriedly explained the situation. "Am I doing something wrong?" she asked. "He cried off and on last night, but I never had to hold the key this long."

"Is he in the right position?"

Leigh double-checked. "Yes."

"Did you drop him or anything?"

"No!"

"Just stay calm, then. Sometimes it can take over thirty minutes."

Leigh cradled the phone under her chin. "I'm doing everything we talked about and—"

"Braghhhh!"

"He cried!" Leigh exclaimed. She took out the key, then clapped her hand over her mouth. "I hope I didn't just wake him up."

Christian laughed. "Good job."

"You're a lifesaver." Suddenly Leigh realized she had no idea why Christian had called. "I'm sorry to have gone on like that. . . ."

Several seconds passed. Leigh got nervous. Why *had* he called her?

"Uh, Leigh?"

"Yes?"

"I wanted to tell you about this show I was watching."

She relaxed. "What is it?"

"A documentary on A&E about the British royal family. I thought you'd like it."

"I'll turn it on. After I put Charlie down, that is."

There was a slight pause. "Well, I guess I'll see you tomorrow."

"Okay." Leigh found herself longing to talk more, but she had nothing to say.

She heard Christian clear his throat. "Leigh?"

"Yes?"

"Could you, uh, could you believe that scene in the assembly the other day? I thought steam was going to burst out of Mrs. Bauer's head, she was so angry."

Leigh giggled, carefully placing Charlie back on her bed. "I know. But you have to admit that she had a point. When Dave Reynolds stood up and said that Fillmore's art department was filled with burned-out teachers—"

"Hey, he's got the right to his opinion—"

"But he directed it right at Mrs. Bauer!" Leigh objected as Christian went on about the assembly.

"Enough talk about that," Leigh said when he was through. "Tell me about the music scene in England."

"My favorite topic." Christian took a deep breath. "It all begins with an album called *Revolver*. . . ."

Leigh was amazed at how close their taste was in music. From rock to techno to Britpop, they matched. "Do you have to get going?" Leigh asked after about ten minutes, worried she'd kept him on for much too long.

"Not unless you do. When I get a captive audience, I hold them prisoner for as long as I can."

"I'll remember that." Leigh smiled. "So did you go to any raves in London?" she asked.

"A couple. The music was cool, but I'm not into the drug scene, and it was pretty intense."

"I bet."

"Have you ever been to a rave?" Christian asked.

"In my dreams!"

"Well, if there's ever one in Buffalo, we'll go, all right?"

"Um, sure." Shyness overcame her. Did he really mean it?

"Hey," Christian put in excitedly, "did you hear who's coming here next weekend?"

"Who?"

"Oasis."

"I know," Leigh said. "Their attitude needs some adjusting, but I hear they rock in concert. I wish we could go."

"Yeah. They're sold out. In England they sold out majorly fast too."

Leigh giggled. "Every time you mention England, I get this craving for a hot cup of tea."

"Let me warn you, I make a mean cuppa."

"Cuppa?"

"Cup of tea. Cuppa. Guaranteed relaxation."

"I could use it after my episode with Charlie."

"You did fine," Christian assured her. "Oh, wow, is it ten already?"

Leigh glanced at her clock. "Yep."

"Guess I made you miss the documentary," Christian said.

Leigh shrugged happily. "That's okay. I was getting my information directly from the source."

"Happy to inform. Catch you tomorrow."

"Okay."

"Bye," Christian said.

"Bye."

"G'night."

Leigh laughed. "Good night." She hung up.

Christian was just so easy to talk to, to be herself with. There had to be another guy out there that made her feel that way.

Didn't there?

Seven

"I'VE BEEN THINKING a lot about what you said to me the other day," Kerry confided during fourth-period lunch on Tuesday. She stirred her raspberry yogurt.

"And what incredibly smart thing is that?" Leigh asked, taking a big bite of her peanut butter and jelly sandwich. They were at their usual table in the cafeteria with Allison and Lucy, their infant carriers resting side by side.

Kerry took a spoonful of yogurt. "Remember how you were saying that maybe instead of trying to keep doing the same old things together, Christian and I should try something new?"

Leigh nodded.

Kerry whipped out a small envelope from her backpack and pulled out two tickets. "How's *this* for something new?"

Leigh and Lucy leaned across the table to see.

81

"Oasis tickets!" Allison shrieked so loud that people four tables over turned to look. "How'd you score these?"

"Yeah," Lucy said, her blue eyes wide. "I heard they sold out right away!"

Leigh simply stared, her mouth agape.

Kerry beamed. "My mom has this friend who works at the ticket center, and she was able to get them for me. They cost an arm and a leg, but it's worth it."

Leigh ripped open a bag of pretzels. "Does Christian know you've got them?" For some reason she couldn't quite explain, she hadn't told Kerry about her conversation with Christian on Sunday.

Kerry shook her head. "I'm going to surprise him. It's our two-year anniversary. I wanted to do something special." She helped herself to an Oreo from Lucy's tray. "He's going to flip when he finds out."

"He'll be beyond psyched," Lucy agreed.

"You know, I can't believe how good-looking he got since he went away," Allison remarked. She leaned in conspiratorially toward Leigh. "Of course, you never saw him before. He was always a babe, but there must be something in the water over there because he came back even better than he was."

"English guys." Lucy sighed.

Kerry wiped her mouth with her napkin. "Christian's not English, Luce."

"Yeah, English guys are usually skinny with wild haircuts," Allison declared.

"Al!" Leigh laughed.

"What?" Allison flicked a crumb off the table. "Hey, I'm not saying that's bad or anything. I think it's kind of sexy. But English girls probably weren't used to seeing guys like Christian. He's so cute and funny, and, well, built."

"Going to a concert with him is a great idea," Lucy confirmed. "Standing in the dark listening to cool music—the perfect romantic setting. Especially if you guys are having trouble."

Allison nodded in agreement and picked up her tray as the bell rang. "Gotta book."

"I wanted to ask you a favor," Kerry said to Leigh as they filed out of the cafeteria, carriers in tow.

"Sure, what?"

"Well, you and Christian are spending a lot of time together because of this baby program."

"Yes . . . ?"

"I was thinking about what Allison was saying about English girls. Maybe Christian *did* meet someone in England. Someone he liked better than me."

"You think?" Leigh frowned. "But you guys agreed to tell each other if you met somebody else. If he hasn't said anything, then I'm sure he didn't. Christian seems really honest, Kerry."

"He is," Kerry admitted, chewing her lip.

Leigh stopped to get a drink at the fountain.

"But would it hurt you to do a little innocent meddling?" Kerry continued, a hopeful expression on her face.

"Aw, Kerry, I don't want to get involved."

Kerry held up her hands. "What involved? All

you do is hint around about fidelity and loyalty and stuff and see if he spills anything about last year. And then"—Kerry tossed back her hair—"then you can see if he says anything about how he feels about me now."

"Well . . ." Leigh knew there was no way to dodge Kerry once she got stuck on something. "Okay. But I'm not going to be pushy. I don't want him to think I'm some nosy busybody."

Kerry smiled happily. "Better you than me. Thank you *so* much."

"Yeah, sure." Leigh tilted her head toward her math classroom. "I wanna get to class early— Franklin might spring a pop quiz."

"Okay. See you later."

As the girls parted ways on the second floor Leigh wondered if Kerry was taking the right approach. Kerry might be convinced that prying into Christian's life was a good idea, but Leigh wasn't so sure. He seemed like he'd been pretty up-front so far; Christian didn't act like he was a guy with secrets to hide.

And, Leigh thought guiltily as she walked along the hallway, she should know about secrets—because she was keeping a small one herself. One that had to do with how she was feeling lately about Christian.

She wasn't blind. She knew Christian was Kerry's boyfriend—the boyfriend she'd talked about, dreamed about, and obsessed about for the past year. No secret there. And Leigh was happy to see her friend in love.

Except, from what Kerry was saying and what Leigh was seeing, it didn't seem like Kerry was too much in love at all. Hadn't Kerry told her and her friends over and over again how things were different? How Christian had changed in his year abroad? Or that she had changed? Or that *something* had changed?

It was these questions, these moments of doubt, that gave Leigh a little window of shameful hope.

Because the more she heard Kerry talk about her disintegrating relationship with Christian, the more a teeny, tiny part of Leigh wondered if the kernel of attraction she'd felt the moment she'd seen him could grow into anything at all.

There were pinpoints of connections in her mind—dancing with Christian at Kerry's house; eating wings and telling jokes at Jerry's; opening the door to find him standing on her doorstep, his slicker wet with rain, soft brown locks of hair lying damp on his forehead; laughing with him on the phone.

Leigh slammed the mental window shut. There was no use dreaming about things that could never come true . . . things that would only hurt someone she loved.

Leigh pushed her wobbly old desk next to Christian's, and Kerry and Jason joined them. They'd handed in the dolls at the beginning of class and now they were working in groups of four. For the first few minutes they were diligent students, copying down the notes Mrs. Duncan had placed on the blackboard and sharing their results with one another. But when Mrs. Duncan joined another group's discussion, they began to slack off.

"Everybody's been talking about the Oasis concert this weekend," Christian said. "I heard they were giving tickets away this past weekend."

Leigh glanced over at Kerry—she was doing a great job of keeping a poker face.

"Yeah, I know," Jason groused. "I spent four hours trying to call up and win on Friday."

"Their last album was the best," Leigh said, winking to Kerry to give her the perfect lead-in.

Kerry smiled. "Well, it was supposed to be a—"

Christian reached in his back pocket and casually tossed two tickets onto the table. *"Soo-prise,"* he drawled.

Kerry's jaw dropped. "You've gotta be kidding me."

Christian beamed. "I knew you really wanted to go, and I was able to score these from a friend who can't make the show."

"But you don't understand—I bought us tickets too. That was my soo-prise," she said weakly. Then she snapped her fingers. "I know—we'll scalp 'em. We can make some good money."

"Scalp 'em? Are you nuts?" Jason squeaked. He put his hand over the tickets. "These babies are mine. I'll cough up the cash." He fanned them toward Leigh. "Wanna go halvsies?"

Leigh looked uncertainly at Kerry. "You guys wouldn't mind?"

"Mind? It'll be awesome!" Christian exclaimed. "Besides, scalping is a pain. And I know"—he hesitated—"I know how much you like them."

Leigh watched as the prospect of a romantic concert for two drained out of Kerry's face, leaving her cheeks pale and her eyes full of disappointment.

"Christian's right," Kerry said faintly after a few seconds, her lips curving into a small smile. She studied the tickets. "And they're all on the floor, so that's good. We can—"

"Are we talking or are we working?" Mrs. Duncan asked smoothly, stopping by their desks.

"Now what would you expect from parents like us?" Christian asked.

The library was pretty crowded Wednesday afternoon, but then it always was during last-period study hall. After checking all her favorite spots for seats, Leigh and Christian finally settled down at one of the large tables next to the reference section.

Leigh curled her legs up under her Indian style and began organizing her materials into little piles. "Okay, I've got my daily journal and my handbook."

"And I've got the instruction sheets Mrs. Duncan wanted us to fill out." Christian pulled a spiral notebook out of his backpack.

"Now, we're supposed to hand in our journals so she can see if our comments match up with the databases in the dolls." Leigh peeked over at Christian's log. "Your handwriting is so neat for a guy."

Christian wrote his name on one of the instruction sheets. "Yeah, it just takes me an hour to think of what I want to say."

"Really?" Leigh scanned down the list of questions. "This looks pretty easy, though. Take number four—'What types of skills or personality traits are important for new parents to have?'" She began to count off a list on her fingers. "Patience, energy, love—"

"Money," Christian put in.

"Money?" Leigh cast him a wary glance.

"You know, to pay the baby-sitter when the key won't work."

"Christian!"

He held up his hands. "I'm serious. When we were at the mall with the dolls, Kerry and I stopped in the drugstore to check the price of diapers. They cost over eight dollars a box!" He wrinkled his nose. "And do you have any idea how many diapers the average baby goes through in a week? It's pretty gross."

"True. Babies are expensive." As part of their assignment, they were supposed to price baby necessities like formula and diapers. Before she had visited Baby & Co. Furniture, Leigh had no idea a crib could cost so much. "But," she added, "they're cute." She nibbled on her pen. "You're right, though. The ability to earn enough money to support a baby is really important."

They went through the rest of the questions. When the end-of-school bell rang at two-forty, Leigh was shocked. The period had flown by! Working with Christian didn't seem like work at all—it was fun. He kept telling funny stories that sent her into fits of giggles, but in between all the laughing and kidding around they'd managed to accomplish a lot.

"Did you want to get going?" Christian asked, tilting his head toward the steel-rimmed clock that loomed over them.

"The library is open another hour," Leigh said. Christian didn't seem like he was in a hurry to leave, and they'd worked so well together today, it seemed a shame to call it quits. "I can stay if you want."

Christian nodded. "Might as well keep going. The more we get done now, the less we'll need to do later." He stood up and stretched. "I've got a stash of apples in my locker. Want one?"

"Okay." Making sure nothing valuable was left for grabs on the table, Christian and Leigh walked out the library's glass doors and down the stairs toward the pool, where Christian's locker was. The halls were already pretty empty—people didn't stick around long once the final bell rang.

Christian spun his lock's combination. "It feels kind of weird to be without little Charlie."

Leigh giggled. "Doesn't it? I couldn't believe how much work it was to take care of him."

The lock released, and Christian opened the door. Although it wasn't as done up as hers, Christian had decorated his locker too. A Buffalo Bills logo was affixed to the door, a Prodigy decal was stuck to the back, and a bright blue terry cloth towel with the words *Crystal Palace* on it hung from a movable magnetic hook.

Christian took two apples off the shelf and handed one to Leigh. "Freshly picked."

"By you?" Leigh loved going apple picking. She'd gone to one of the orchards in Fredonia, south of Buffalo, last year with her dad. They'd picked a bushel of apples and bought several quarts of the tangy, purple-skinned grapes Leigh had soon become addicted to. There wasn't anything like them where she'd grown up in California.

"Yup. My mom dragged my sister, Emily, and me along on Sunday." Then he flashed a huge grin. "It wasn't that bad, though. Em can be a pain, but deep down she really missed her charming older bro. She made my mom buy Cocoa Pebbles last week, and she knows that I'm the only one who eats the stuff." He put his hand on his heart. "It was beautiful."

"That's really cute." Leigh didn't know too many guys who willingly did things with their families and liked it. In fact, she didn't think she knew any at all. "I bet you're a cool big brother," she said out of the blue.

"Really? Why?" Christian's hazel eyes flickered with curiosity.

Leigh chomped into her apple as they headed back upstairs. "I don't know. You're sweet and funny. And you've been to Europe and stuff, and I would have loved to have had someone like you to tell me all about it."

"All Em was interested in was the fake tiara and shortbread cookies I brought her." He slam-dunked his apple core into the trash can that sat outside the library. "I'm pretty glad to be back home, though. I got kind of homesick in the end. . . . It was great to see my parents and Emily again. And Kerry too," he added.

"What were the kids our age like there?" Leigh asked as they entered the library and returned to their seats.

"Pretty cool. I hung out a lot with Simon and his friends," Christian explained as he opened his handbook. "Being with him was a great way to meet people."

"Did you meet lots of girls?" Leigh asked.

"Sure."

His easy response startled her for a moment. Maybe fishing for information for Kerry wouldn't be too hard after all. She began to shuffle her papers on the table. "I mean, any girls you, um, liked?" She could feel Christian looking at her.

"Why do you ask?" Christian teased. "Interested?"

Leigh was mortified. "No!" She quickly picked up her notebook and haphazardly began thumbing through it. Then she put it down. "I can't believe you said that!"

"Sorry," Christian said sheepishly. "I guess I had enough of Kerry grilling me the other night. Kidding's the only way not to let it get to me."

"What do you mean?" Leigh put down her notebook and glanced over at the librarians' desk. Now that school was officially over for the day, they could talk and not have to worry about getting in trouble.

Christian shrugged. "She's just been asking me a lot of questions about what I did there. With girls, that is."

"Guess she's just curious." Leigh toyed with her topaz ring. "Girls love guys with British accents, and maybe she thought you felt the same way about the girls there or something. I mean, English girls," she finished lamely. *What am I saying? I sound like a total idiot.*

He laughed. "I met girls with English accents, Irish accents, and American accents. There were five other Americans studying at my school."

"Oh." It hadn't occurred to Leigh that Christian wouldn't be the only American at Lellington. She shouldn't have brought up the dating thing. It was none of her business, and the easy rapport they'd developed had disappeared. Now she felt uncomfortable. "We should get back to work if we're going to stay here," Leigh said, picking up her pen.

"Wait a second." Christian reached over and put his hand on her paper. "I didn't date anybody there, if that's what you're asking me." He sighed. "Simon's clique includes a lot of girls: Emma, Jane, Neera. . . . They were nice girls. We had fun." His hazel eyes grew serious. "But Kerry and I made a promise to each other, and I kept it." He colored slightly, his eyes flickering uncertainly to Leigh's. "But now . . ."

"Now?"

Christian let out a slow groan. "I don't know. Things are—things are different, that's all."

She gazed into his eyes. "How?"

"I guess I probably shouldn't be telling you this," Christian began, a guilty look on his face.

"You're her best friend and all, and—"

"Kerry's afraid you met someone else," Leigh blurted out. She knew Kerry would have preferred a more subtle approach, but she didn't know when she'd have such a good opportunity again.

Christian stared down at the floor. "I wish it were that easy."

Leigh grew suddenly cold, wrapping her arms around herself. "Well, have you . . . met someone?" she whispered, not sure she wanted an answer.

"No, well, I don't know." Christian rocked back and forth in his chair. "Kerry's great. It's just that I—I—" He broke off, putting his head in his hands. "I don't know. I guess I need time to think."

"Sure," Leigh said, nodding. A dull, unwelcome lump had settled in her stomach. She'd never in a million years believed that Kerry's fears about Christian were true. And maybe they weren't. Christian sure wasn't shedding much light on the subject. She'd nodded as if she understood where he was coming from, but she didn't at all. Either he loved Kerry or he didn't. Either way, Leigh shouldn't have butted in. She couldn't possibly tell Kerry what Christian had said without devastating her.

"Leigh?" He looked straight into her eyes. "Please don't tell Kerry all of this. I don't want to upset her."

"Well, I wouldn't know what to say anyway," Leigh said.

With a wry smile Christian shut his notebook. "That makes two of us."

Eight

GAS STATIONS, BURGER joints, Irish pubs. A sea of neon lights flashed by as Leigh's school bus bumped down the road on Friday afternoon. Sometimes her mom picked her up from school, and sometimes she caught a ride with Jason or Kerry, but mostly she had to rely on the good old orange limousine.

Leigh tried to get comfortable in the ripped vinyl seat, but comfortable and bus didn't go together. Most of the other student riders she was friendly with had gotten off already, and now it was just her and a few stragglers left for the rest of the ride. Her thoughts floated back to the conversation she'd had with Christian in the library. It had been so confusing—there was nothing reassuring she could pull from it to tell Kerry. Now she was going to have to play dumb if Kerry brought it up.

Being dishonest with her best friend was the

worst, and Leigh was beginning to hate herself more and more each day. Because with each day that passed, she'd been allowing herself the guilty luxury of thinking about Christian as more than a friend.

It seemed as if they were always running into each other in the hallways at school. She'd see him at his locker when she arrived in the morning. He'd pass by when she was on the way to English and he was on the way to physics. Everything was completely platonic, but somehow along the way, Leigh had begun to develop, well, feelings for Christian. Feelings that she'd never had before, for anyone else.

Feelings that scared her.

There was absolutely, positively no way she would ever, *ever* go after a friend's boyfriend, especially a friend like Kerry. She'd never even go after an enemy's boyfriend! There were plenty of unattached guys to like. Why mess around with someone who already had another half? And besides, any guy who would cheat on his girlfriend to be with someone else would have to be a loser anyway. And trust a guy who did? Forget it.

But the way she felt about Christian had made Leigh question everything she'd ever felt for someone of the opposite sex. Sure, when she'd first seen him, Leigh had thought he was gorgeous. But when she'd found out who he was, all PG, PG-13, and okay, R-rated thoughts of him had immediately been erased from her brain.

Until Kerry had told her things were rocky.

Until Christian had told her things were very rocky.

And then it was impossible to keep her heart from opening up any longer.

"Your stop, Feralano!" barked one of the boys who sat in the back of the bus.

Leigh hurriedly gathered her things and scooted down the bus's steps.

In reality, nothing had changed. Kerry and Christian were still going out, and Kerry was still Leigh's best friend in the world.

And I'm going to do everything in my power to make sure Kerry and Christian work things out, Leigh promised herself fiercely as she bolted up the sidewalk to her back door. Because, she rationalized, that was the only way she could be forgiven if she did the unthinkable.

If she allowed herself to fall in love with beautiful, wonderful Christian Archer.

Leigh had filled in for Rochelle today from ten to six at the Sweater Set, and by the time she'd punched out, raced home, showered, and eaten dinner, she'd had exactly nine minutes before a horn beeped outside her house.

Taking one last harried look in the mirror, Leigh shoved fifteen dollars into her pocket, dabbed on some lip gloss, and ran down the stairs.

"You look cute, honey," her mom said. She tapped a piece of scrap paper on the counter. "This is the number of the restaurant Dad and I will be at, and we might drop by the Chisholms' for a drink. We should be home by twelve." She brushed some imaginary lint off Leigh's shoulders. "Have a good time. Tell Christian to drive safely."

"I will." This was the first year Leigh had been allowed to ride in a car with a teenage driver at night. It felt great not to be always chauffeured around like a baby.

Leigh gave her mom a quick hug, grabbed her coat from the hall closet, and was out the door just in time for the horn's second round of beeps.

The door to Christian's Chrysler opened and a wave of Beck greeted her.

"Hi, guys!" she shouted over the pulsing beat.

Kerry grinned from the front seat. "Get ready to rock and roll, Feralano."

The concert was being held in the Aud, a huge venue in downtown Buffalo.

"You'd think they'd get this down after a while," Jason grumbled as the four of them wedged through the crowded ticket holders entrance and spilled out into the food concession area.

Leigh nodded, clutching her ticket so tightly, it was beginning to warp. She felt like a sardine.

"And don't even think about peeing," Kerry said, thumbing toward the bathrooms. Already the line was filled with about thirty desperate-looking girls. As usual, the men's room had no line whatsoever.

"Hey! Look who's here." Christian pointed to the concession stand.

Leigh and Kerry turned to see a group of three boys carrying skateboards and wearing baggy pants and T-shirts standing in line. They were shoving each other back and forth and badgering a group of girls in front of them.

"Tim!" Kerry shrieked. Her eyes narrowed into little slits. "This must be a nightmare."

At the sound of Kerry's voice Tim turned. He and his friends made a beeline for them.

"Hey, Christian, Jason," Tim said, slapping the guys five.

Kerry folded her arms across her chest. "Why are you here?"

"There's this concert tonight, right? It's this really cool group, Oasis, who—"

Kerry grabbed Tim roughly by the shoulder. "Cut it out, buttface. Does Mom know you're here?"

"Take it easy, man." Tim made a big show of rubbing his shoulder. "That woman Mom knows at the ticket place got extra tickets. You guys had already left. Dad just dropped us off."

"You mean you guys are here all alone?" Leigh asked. Her parents hadn't let her go to a concert unsupervised until this year.

"Yeah. Dad said if we saw you, we should ask Christian if we can get a ride home with you guys, then call home and leave a message."

Christian tossed his keys in the air and caught them behind his back. "Sure, if you don't mind sitting on someone's lap."

"If I can sit on Kerry's," Tim's friend Justin said, batting his eyelashes.

She raised her eyebrows. "In your dreams."

"Come on, we should head down into the arena," Jason said, starting to move forward. The stadium was really starting to fill up.

"We wanted to get pretzels!" Tim complained.

"Forget it," Kerry barked.

Leigh kept an eye on Jason's red ski jacket as it wove through the crowd. She quickened her pace, not wanting to lose him.

"Are you guys coming?" she said, looking back over her shoulder.

"We're right behind you!" Christian shouted over the crowd. "Just keep moving. We need to get to door 112—that'll take us down to the floor."

By this point Leigh could no longer turn around—there were too many people pushing against her. The sounds of the opening band drifted out into the corridors. She wished they had left an hour earlier.

Finally they were at door 112, where they had to go through single file and show the usher their tickets before proceeding down a narrow flight of steps.

Leigh reached forward and managed to tug on Jason's sleeve. "Jason, wait for everybody to catch up." A second or so later she spotted Christian. Leigh and Jason leaned against the railing and let a bunch of people pass.

"Phew! It's like a cattle herd out there," Christian declared once he reached them. "I've got to get this off." He pulled off his navy blue sweatshirt. Underneath was a ribbed formfitting T-shirt.

It fit his form perfectly.

Leigh adjusted her scrunchie. "Where's Kerry?"

"She's right behind me." Christian peered back up into the crowd.

"You can't stand here," barked a security guard from behind him.

"We're waiting for our friend," Christian explained.

"Well, you gotta wait down there, then." The guard gestured down to the floor. Hundreds of people were milling around.

"But she'll never find us down there!" Leigh protested, staring down at the sea of heads. "We've got to go back out there."

The guard held up his hands. "Not if you want to see the concert, you don't. Didn't you hear the announcement? Once you're on the floor, there's no readmittance if you leave."

"What if you've got to use the john?" Jason asked, incredulous.

"They've got 'em down there."

"What should we do?" Christian asked.

Leigh gazed back up through the crowd, and Jason stood as tall as he could, looking from left to right. After a few minutes he shook his head. "No sign of her, man."

"Come on, people, get moving," the security guard grumbled.

Christian let out a frustrated sigh. "I don't see her either. Guess we don't have a choice." He motioned for Leigh to go in front of him.

100

"What could have happened to her?" Leigh wailed as the opening band broke into their next song. People were pushing in on all sides.

"I don't get it." Christian's brow was creased with worry as they reached the floor. "Kerry and the boys were right beside me, then all of a sudden they weren't."

Exasperated, Jason ran his fingers through his hair. "At least we have the meeting point outside when the concert's through."

Leigh nodded. Thank God they'd thought to set that up.

"Well, we'll keep looking for her," Christian said as they began to inch their way through the thickening throng.

Leigh shoved her hands in her back pockets. "Maybe she'll find us," she said, straining to be heard above the noisy din.

"Yeah, we look so different from anybody else here," Christian attempted to joke.

With a sinking feeling, Leigh realized Christian was right. She tried to scan the faces of the concertgoers as they made their way down the staircase. But it was impossible to make anyone out. And then without warning, the stadium went black.

A roar came up from the crowd. The concert was going to begin.

"Come on," Christian said finally, taking her hand and pulling her forward. Out of nowhere, a rush of excitement shot through her at his touch. "We came here to have fun, right?"

"Right," Leigh said through a smoky haze, allowing herself to be pulled into the horde of screaming fans, her hand held safely in Christian's.

"Cool concert, man," Jason said, his head still bopping to the music. "That guitar player wailed!"

Leigh didn't respond. She was too busy searching the crowd for a familiar blond ponytail. *What if she's not at the meeting point? We can't just leave here without—*

Suddenly Leigh felt a sharp tug on her jacket. "Hey!" she exclaimed, spinning around. "Kerry!" Waves of relief washed over her.

Kerry just stood there, arms crossed. "Nice, guys."

"We are *so* sorry," Leigh began, trying to ignore the expression of pure fury on Kerry's face. If she'd hear them out, give them a chance to explain—

Kerry just glowered.

"I know you're mad at us, but it really wasn't our fault," Christian began.

"You guys totally ditched me!" Kerry burst out. "In case you didn't notice, I had to spend the whole concert with my idiot baby brother and his moronic friends."

"We tried to go and look for you," Jason told her. "The guard wouldn't let us out."

"I bet if you'd given him ten bucks, he would've!" Kerry said, her voice shaking.

Leigh felt awful. Any enjoyment she'd had was

being replaced by sadness at what Kerry was going through.

"Where did you go?" Christian asked, his voice full of concern.

"We searched the whole floor for you," Leigh added.

"All I know is that I stopped for one lousy second and when I looked up, you guys had vanished!" Kerry said. A tear trickled down her face.

"I'm sorry," Christian apologized, trying to wipe her cheek. Kerry angrily brushed his hand away. "The last thing I saw was you—right behind me. And then you were gone." Christian moved over to the side, out of the path of exiting concertgoers. Leigh, Kerry, and Jason followed suit. "Where's Tim?"

Kerry gestured to the souvenir stand. Her brother and his friends were having a heated discussion on what was better value for the money: T-shirts or baseball caps.

"So we got separated," Christian said softly. "At least we found each other now."

"So we got separated?" Kerry repeated, her voice thick with emotion. "Tonight was supposed to be for our anniversary, Christian."

He shifted his feet. "I know, but—"

"And I come over to you guys and you're all talking like you don't even care about me."

Leigh reached over and touched her arm. "You know that's not true. We weren't allowed to leave the floor—what could we have done?"

Kerry pulled on her gloves and zipped up her coat. "I just want to go home."

Christian headed for the souvenir stand. "I'll round these three up."

"Did you at least enjoy the concert?" Leigh asked, anxious to find something positive about the evening. "I thought they were pretty good. . . ."

Kerry shrugged. Her eyes flashed toward Christian. "I know you guys didn't mean to lose me. But this really sucks big-time."

Leigh squeezed her shoulder sympathetically.

The silence as the seven of them walked through the parking lot to Christian's car was deafening. Even Tim and his friends were quiet.

"Anybody in the mood for Jerry's?" Jason asked once everyone was squeezed in.

"That could be fun," Christian said, turning to Kerry in the seat beside him. "Ker?"

"Yeah, maybe you guys could all get a table and when I go to the bathroom, you can leave."

"Good idea!" Tim cracked from the backseat. "Why didn't I ever think of it?" His friends hooted.

"Cut it out, guys," Christian warned, pulling out of the lot. "Are you sure you don't want to come?" he asked Kerry again.

"Positive." She closed her eyes. "Besides, I've got that color guard competition in Syracuse tomorrow. The bus leaves at seven."

Leigh settled back in the seat as Christian drove along the highway. She felt horrible just for losing

Kerry for a couple of hours—how could she live with herself if anything went on between her and Christian? Sure, holding his hand for that brief moment at the concert's beginning had given her chills like nothing else ever had. But she could never allow herself to have feelings for him.

Never, ever, she vowed.

That would ruin everything.

By the time they reached Kerry's house, Leigh had heard about twenty stupid jokes from Tim and his crew. And all right, she had laughed at a few of them. But Kerry hadn't even cracked a smile. Leigh had stared woefully at the back of Kerry's blond-ponytailed head for miles.

After saying their good-byes, Jason moved up to the front seat and Leigh stretched out in the back, grateful for the extra legroom.

Christian's expression was grim as he drove back down Kerry's long, winding street out to the main road. "I can't believe that happened. How can you lose someone at a concert?"

"It is unbelievable," Leigh said.

Jason sighed. "At least the music was good."

Christian popped a cassette in the car stereo, turning the volume up so loud that talking was virtually impossible. Leigh guessed he wanted it that way. What was there to say?

When they dropped Jason off a few minutes later, Leigh climbed in the front seat. She was silent as Christian drove down the boulevard.

Glancing over at him, she saw that he had a tiny hole in his earlobe.

"Do you have your ear pierced?" she asked.

"Yeah."

"How come I've never noticed it?"

"I don't wear an earring that often. Kerry hates it."

"Oh."

"Do you like guys with earrings?"

She'd always found guys who wore earrings—nothing dumb or dangly, just a plain, simple stud—sexy. Leigh fidgeted with the ticket stubs in her lap. "Kind of," she allowed.

"Hmmm." Christian took out the tape and turned on the radio instead. She noticed that his fingernails were extrathick.

"You must drink lots of milk," she blurted.

He looked at her questioningly.

"Your fingernails," Leigh said sheepishly. "They're so white. See how weak and brittle mine are?" She held up her hand. "They break all the time."

"Really?" With his right hand Christian reached over and put his nails over hers, pressing slightly. "They don't feel weak."

Leigh swallowed hard. "Yeah, well, they are."

Christian moved his fingertips down so that they were lightly touching hers. "You have nice hands," he said.

"You too." Her heart was beating so fast, she was sure Christian could hear every thump. She'd never been so glad to see her street sign. "There's my house," Leigh said, pulling her hand away and pointing to her brick split-level, lit only by the timed light in the living room.

Christian nodded. "I was here last week, remember?"

"Oh, that's right." Leigh's fingertips were tingling. She forced them to lie still on her lap.

Christian pulled up to the front of the house and shifted into park. "Some night, huh?"

"I had fun," Leigh said.

"Me too. Some concerts don't live up to your expectations, but this one was excellent."

"Mmmm."

"Except for—"

"Yeah," Leigh said quickly.

For a moment Leigh thought of inviting Christian in. She didn't relish the idea of being home alone at night, even if it was only for an hour or two. Then she decided against it. Christian was probably anxious to get home. "Well, thanks for the ride," she said, opening the door and hopping out.

"I'll wait till you get in."

Leigh flashed him one last smile. "Thanks."

As she hurried up the walk to her house she ran her thumb over her fingertips. She knew it wasn't her imagination that Christian's fingers had lingered just a little too long on hers. Not that fingertips were the sexiest body part or anything, but it was the *way* he'd touched her. . . .

Opening the screen door, Leigh's eyes filled with sudden tears. How could she be so shameful? How could *she*, of all people, even want to touch

Christian Archer's fingertips, especially after what had happened to Kerry's plans for a romantic evening? After she'd vowed only minutes earlier to write him off?

And how could she go on pretending things were normal now that she had?

Nine

LEIGH LOVED AUTUMN Sundays. Church followed by a late morning brunch with her parents, curling up on the sofa with a good book, taking a nap in front of the fireplace. Or enjoying one of her most favorite activities of all: sleeping in.

Which was exactly what she was doing this particular Sunday morning when the phone rang.

"Leigh!" her mom's voice called, sounding especially harsh to Leigh's still asleep brain. Normally she dove for the phone, but at this hour she'd been positive it wasn't for her. None of her friends made phone calls before noon, and everybody knew she would've had a late night at the concert.

"Hello?" she mumbled, clicking on the cordless. Her hair, fanned out on her pillow, reeked of smoke, and her voice crackled in her ears, hoarse from all the singing she'd done last night.

"Leigh?"

It was a guy. Leigh sat up straight. "Uh-huh?"

"Hey, it's Christian. Did I wake you?"

The memory of her hand in his came back to her then, thrilling and scaring her at the same time. "N-No," she stammered, rubbing the sleep out of her eyes. Then she yawned. "Well, yes."

"Your voice sounds almost as bad as mine did this morning," Christian said.

Leigh swallowed, wishing she had a glass of water. "I still can't believe what happened last night," Leigh lamented, rubbing her temples.

"I know." A few seconds of silence passed. Then Christian spoke up again. "Leigh?"

"Yes?"

"Take a look outside."

Leigh peered through her miniblinds. Bright cheery sunlight spilled across the wide front lawn, making her squint.

"If you thought you'd tp'd my house after you dropped me off last night, you picked the wrong one," she grumbled good-naturedly.

Christian laughed. "It's such a great day out, I was wondering if you'd want to drive up to Niagara Falls."

Leigh rolled out of her cherry sleigh bed, tucking the phone in the crook of her neck. "You talked Kerry into going up there?" she asked. Kerry hated the falls. "Nothing but a tourist trap," she'd pronounced dismissively when Leigh had suggested they make a day of it there last summer.

"No—she's twirling flags at that color guard competition, remember?"

"Oh, right," Leigh recalled, still a little bleary-eyed. Yawning, she stretched her arms and raised the blind that framed her large bedroom window. "So . . . you mean . . . you just want to go with me?" she asked. The thought made her slightly nauseous.

Christian chuckled. "Gee, don't give yourself so much credit."

"Well, um, do you think Kerry would mind?"

"No, I called her up last night when I got home to apologize one more time and told her I might ask you to go—a change of pace from studying at the library. She said to have fun."

"Oh." Leigh's cheeks began to burn. Obviously Christian didn't have any romantic inclinations for her—this was nothing more than a glorified study session. And she felt like a traitorous idiot for having any for him. *If I don't go because I'm afraid I'm starting to like him, that's worse than actually going and proving that I have no interest in him whatsoever. Isn't it?*

"I just thought that since you'd mentioned once that you'd never been there and since we still have some loose ends to tie up on our health project . . ." Christian let the rest of the sentence hang.

Leigh couldn't decide. Should she say yes? Studying together at the library or going over stuff at her house was one thing . . . but to actually go on a trip together to Niagara Falls? To Canada?

"Being in the library on a day like today seems so beat," Christian added.

It wasn't like going to Niagara Falls alone with Christian was a *date* or anything.

111

That would be totally ridiculous.

And if Kerry was cool with it . . .

"Okay, I'm up for it," Leigh decided.

"All right! Pick you up in thirty?"

Leigh caught a glimpse of herself in the mirror. Frightening. "Sixty."

"Welcome to Canada. *Bienvenue au Canada,*" Leigh said, reading the words on the huge sign that greeted them as Christian pulled off the Rainbow Bridge. "This is so fabulous!"

Christian smiled over at her, the flecks in his hazel eyes accentuated by the bulky navy-and-brown sweater he wore. "Good thing I didn't tell the customs guy about the dead body in the trunk."

"Guess they wouldn't go for that." Leigh wrapped her arms around herself. "Do you know that this is the first foreign country I've been to?" She closed her eyes. "I know this is probably no big thrill for you, but I'm actually tingling."

Christian made a sudden turn. "I'll give you the tour of the city before we park."

Leigh gazed impatiently out the window as they drove past a gigantic gambling casino and up Clifton Hill, a narrow, winding street. She'd never seen so many tourist attractions crammed into such a tiny square footage. The Movieland Wax Museum. Guinness Book of World Records. Ripley's Believe It or Not! Museum. Everywhere she looked, signs were blinking. Hotel rooms with heart-shaped beds! Pancakes and bacon for $2.50! Iguanas that talk!

"Did you say beautiful?" Leigh pointed to a wax museum touting the world's shortest married couple, a bargain at only five dollars admission.

"Cheesy can be beautiful in its own way," Christian maintained. "But you haven't seen the falls yet, California, so you just keep quiet."

"Okay, but you'd better not let me down."

Leigh settled back happily in her seat. Who would've guessed you could get along so well with a guy you'd only known for two weeks? It felt like much, much longer. Maybe it had something to do with all she'd heard about him before he'd arrived. But then, she'd heard a lot about other things before, like how cold Buffalo winters were, and that hadn't made those any easier to take.

She was pleased that they'd managed to get a lot of work done on the drive up: Leigh had read aloud the journal entries she'd kept, and they'd decided on who would speak about what during the ten-minute class presentation they would be giving in class on Thursday.

They coasted back down the hill then and drove off to the left. At the hill's base the businesses and stores were fewer, but the pedestrians and cars were plenty. After driving around for twenty minutes trying to find a spot alongside the road, Christian finally gave up and parked the Chrysler in one of the tiny parking lots that charged ten dollars an hour.

"Sorry," he apologized. "I forgot how crowded it gets."

Leigh shut her door. "I'm just glad we're here."

113

Niagara Falls was only about thirty minutes from Leigh's house. How could she have lived in Buffalo a whole year without visiting it?

The air felt cool and crisp on Leigh's cheeks. Clumps of early morning fog still lingered over patches of damp grass, and the sun was peeking out from behind the clouds.

"Are you hungry?" Christian asked as they crossed the parking lot. "We can stop and get a muffin or something."

Leigh had managed to scarf down a toaster strudel and two bowls of cereal before Christian had picked her up. "I'll be okay," she told him. "Now that we're here, I just want to get to the falls already!"

Ahead of them lay Queen Victoria Park, a gigantic expanse of land lined with small boulders and long furrows of rich-looking dirt that Leigh imagined housed a host of flowers in the spring and summer. The trees had just started to turn color, and the grass was still a glorious green. Little benches surrounded by wooden buckets of buttery gold mums dotted the sidewalk, and men carrying dust brooms efficiently whisked up cigarette butts and candy wrappers.

"The Canadian side is definitely the best," Christian said, gesturing broadly in front of them. "This side has the Horseshoe Falls. Plus the Canadians have taken a lot better care of their end of things. They've got the tourist stuff, but they've kept the area around the falls pretty pure."

Leigh nodded. Everyone else must've felt the

same way because the path they were walking on was getting packed.

Soon Leigh began to feel a light mist on her face. "Darn, I forgot my umbrella," she muttered. "I thought for sure it was going to be a nice day."

Christian laughed. "The water you feel isn't rain—it's the falls. It always gets misty right before you get to the railings at the edge."

"Oh," Leigh said.

The sound of the falls was amazing, much louder than Leigh had imagined. It was kind of like thunder, booming over and over again. When they reached the railing, Leigh leaned over, trying to take it all in.

"Wow," she breathed as a cool *whish* of water danced over her face. Below, foamy crests boomed and crashed on the rocks. "This is unreal."

"Yeah, it's something." Christian stared out ahead of him. "I guess I take this place for granted, you know, living so close all my life. Sometimes I forget just how amazing it is."

Despite Leigh's protests Christian flagged down a nearby couple to take their picture with his camera. "To remember your first foreign excursion," he said, putting an arm around her and drawing her close. Leigh pushed a soggy strand of hair from her eyes and tried to smile.

As Christian thanked the couple Leigh turned back to the falls. "Ooh, what's that?" she asked, pointing. Down below was what looked to be a tiny log, bobbing up and down into the water.

"That's the *Maid of the Mist*. A tourist boat.

Takes you right underneath the falls," Christian explained. "And you know, no trip to the falls is complete without riding it."

"Is that so?" Leigh asked, grinning. "Then *Maid of the Mist,* here we come!"

After waiting in line to purchase tickets, they had to stand in another line for an elevator that would take them to the dock at Clifton Hill, where they would board the boat. Leigh tried not to notice how rickety everything seemed.

When they finally boarded the elevator and disembarked below, the sound of the water was even more deafening.

"Here!" said a dark-haired woman standing on the entrance ramp to the boat. She handed each of them a blue-hooded rain slicker. "You're gonna need these. One size fits all."

Leigh pulled on the slicker and boarded, being careful not to slip in one of the many puddles that dotted the boat.

"C'mon," said Christian, motioning Leigh to join him.

Leigh stood there, feeling like a little kid, as Christian zipped up her slicker. "There," he said approvingly, tucking in an unruly piece of her hair. Then he looked down at her feet. "Uh-oh. Your shoes will probably get ruined."

"Nah," Leigh said, flexing her toes. "Besides, I've had these loafers for ages. I don't care if they get wet."

Leigh followed Christian past swarms of foreign tourists and mothers tightly holding their squirming

116

children as the boat sputtered to life. Christian politely but firmly elbowed their way forward, and soon they'd found a spot right next to the railing.

A few minutes later they began to move. Water smacked against the boat, and the floor trembled slightly. "I—I don't know if I'm going to like this," Leigh said. "Maybe riding this boat wasn't such a great idea after all."

"You'll be fine," Christian assured her. "I won't let anything happen to you."

Leigh looked up into Christian's warm hazel eyes, and suddenly she was sinking . . . sinking with her feet planted firmly on the sodden wet planks of the boat.

For about the thousandth time that week she found herself wishing with all her might that Christian was single—free to date whoever he wanted.

Free to date her.

But then the rush of who he was came zooming in and she forced herself to come back to earth. No matter how cute he looked in that slicker, his chiseled face framed perfectly by the plasticky blue hood. No matter how many water droplets caught themselves on his impossibly thick, long eyelashes. And no matter how many times he flashed those heartthrob dimples at her, Leigh absolutely could not see him as boyfriend material.

Without warning, the *Maid* lurched forward, and Leigh lost her footing. "Ahh!" she shrieked, sliding forward, arms flailing. All she could see were the huge waves crashing up against the boat, like something out of *Titanic*.

Christian quickly reached out and pulled Leigh close, steadying her. "Whoa, there. Are you okay?"

Leigh nodded. "Just slightly mortified." Kerry had always said that being around Christian gave her the safest feeling in the world. And at that moment, with Christian's arm still around her shoulders, Leigh knew exactly what she meant. "I, uh, panic easily."

"Well, relax. We're getting to the good stuff."

Leigh laid her hand on the railing as they bobbed forward into the Horseshoe Basin and listened as the tour guide described where various people had gone over the falls. "Anna Taylor, a sixty-three-year-old schoolteacher, was the first person to go over the falls in a barrel in 1901. Amazingly, she survived." The guide paused dramatically. "Niagara Falls is one of the seven great wonders of the world," he declared. "Over twelve million guests visit the Canadian side each year."

"And I think they're all on this boat," Christian muttered.

Then suddenly the roar that had been in Leigh's ears for the past ten minutes grew to a deafening crescendo. "And this, ladies and gentlemen, is Niagara Falls!" the guide shouted over the thunderous boom of the waves.

Around them was nothing but roaring, pounding water, soaking their slickers and drenching their feet. Leigh didn't know where the falls ended or the whirlpool they dropped into began—it was one gigantic, booming wet pulse.

"It's incredible!" Leigh shouted above the din.

"I know!" Christian shouted back.

Niagara Falls was nothing like Leigh could have imagined.

And neither was the way her traitorous heart kept racing forward and wouldn't stop . . . no matter how hard she tried to rein it in.

"Here you go," Christian said, handing Leigh a steaming cup of freshly pressed apple cider—or at least that's what the girl behind the counter told him it was. "Wanna grab a seat?"

"Sure," Leigh said. They walked through the main seating area of Over a Barrel, a ski-lodge-theme restaurant. Luckily they nabbed a just vacated table right next to the window, giving themselves a perfect view of the falls in Victoria Park.

Christian took a sip of his drink. "Are you having fun?"

"Are you kidding? This is one of the funnest things I've done all year!" Leigh's eyes skipped around the room and then back out to the falls. "I can't tear my eyes away from them."

"Yeah." Christian knew what that felt like . . . because he was having an awfully hard time tearing his eyes away from her. Leigh looked gorgeous today in her gray wool stretch pants and creamy white lumber jacket, her long hair pulled back into a low ponytail. But it wasn't Leigh's clothes that drew his eye.

It was Leigh herself. The way she tilted her head when she listened to him. The contagious giggle she let erupt every ten seconds. Her enthusiasm to try new things, her willingness to explore the world, the way she cared about people. The relaxed way he felt when he was with her . . .

Sure, Christian admitted to himself as he took another sip of cider, her glossy black hair, beautiful brown eyes, and adorable button nose didn't hurt either. But looks weren't the only thing that mattered—it was how you felt deep down in your gut.

And Christian's gut was telling him that he'd finally found the girl he was meant to be with.

When he'd asked her to come here today, part of him had genuinely just wanted to hang out, to show Leigh the falls and to get some work done for school. But he also couldn't deny that he wanted to be alone with Leigh to give himself a little test . . . a test of the heart. He didn't think he was quite prepared to break up with Kerry. He was afraid—of what, he wasn't sure.

All he knew was that every time he was with Kerry, he felt pressured and tense, and trapped back in tenth grade. *And every time I'm with Leigh, it's anything but. She sees me as the person I am now, not who I used to be.*

"Okay, these are the facts," he mumbled to himself.

"Huh?"

"What?" Christian jumped. Streams of cider began to travel across the table.

"Ooh, let me go get some napkins." Leigh hopped up.

"That's okay. . . ." But she was already halfway toward the counter.

He'd developed the silly habit of talking to himself when he was sightseeing alone in Britain. But he couldn't believe he'd actually done it in front of Leigh. Kicking himself, Christian silently went over everything in his head: He'd gone out with Kerry for a year. They were faithful while they were apart. Now he was back, but he wasn't sure if they should still see each other. He didn't want to hurt anybody. But he was heading toward definite hurt territory. Because he was starting to have feelings—majorly intense feelings—for—

"Why didn't you tell me?" Leigh tossed a pile of thin white napkins on the table.

"Tell you what?" Christian asked, panic-stricken.

"Oh, just that I look like the bride of Frankenstein. I passed by a mirror. My eyes resemble a sick raccoon's. Not to mention my serious hat head."

Christian let out a sigh of relief. "That's all the rage here."

"Lucky for me." Leigh attempted to fluff her hair.

He took a last swallow of cider. "So, is there anything else you want to see?"

"Maybe that tunnel thing where you go behind the falls?" Leigh suggested. They'd passed by a sign advertising it earlier.

"Sounds good."

"Thanks again for bringing me here," Leigh said. Her lips hovered over the steaming cup. "This is one of the best days I've had in a long time."

"Me too," he said, realizing as he said the words how true they were. Spending time with Leigh, hanging out with her, getting to know her—being with this girl made him feel great.

Greater than he ever had with anyone else.

Christian picked up his jacket.

It was like there were all these pieces of his life that had fit together last year before he left. A puzzle with an exact number of pieces and a perfect fit. Somehow, someway, the puzzle had broken apart. And he'd been trying to put it back together again, but the pieces had changed their shape and they didn't fit anymore.

There were new pieces to fit in.

Was Leigh Feralano one of them?

Ten

"COME ON, LADIES. If you don't pick up the pace, you'll be looking at fifty push-ups." Ms. Baker, the girls' butch-haired phys ed teacher, briskly clapped her stubby hands.

"No, *you'd* be looking at fifty push-ups," Kerry said under her breath.

Leigh pushed a disobedient lock of hair off her face as she, Kerry, Allison, and the rest of their sorry-looking gym class began their third lap around the track Monday morning. She already had a painful stitch in her side. Why couldn't they have stayed indoors? The archery targets had been all set up in the indoor gym, but when Baker saw that it was above freezing level outside and that Coach Johnson had the guys out there playing softball, she'd insisted the girls throw on their sweatpants and head to the field.

"What did you do this weekend?" Allison asked Leigh, her green-and-white Fillmore High T-shirt damp with sweat. "Spare me the details about the concert. I already heard how you dumped Kerry."

Leigh shot Kerry a guilty look. "I'm *so* sorry about that."

"Forget it," Kerry said, smiling weakly as they rounded the corner. "I talked with Christian after we got back late last night. He told me you guys had a good time at the falls."

"It's so beautiful there." Leigh paused as they continued to run, trying to forget how cute Christian looked in his rain slicker. "I wish you could've come along."

"We were too busy winning the competition in Syracuse." Kerry grinned. "We were so on."

"Yeah," Allison chimed in. "Even the freshmen hit their marks."

"And did you hear what Mr. Lewis told Jenny?" Kerry asked. "He said that if we keep it up, we might get to go to the Macy's Thanksgiving Day Parade next year!"

"That would be so cool," Allison said, wiping the steam from her glasses.

The girls had now reached the midpoint section of the track, sufficiently far enough from Baker to slow their pace and really talk. "Are you okay, Leigh?" Kerry asked. "You look preoccupied."

Leigh shrugged, bending down to massage her aching calf muscles. The truth was, she couldn't stop thinking about Christian—about the great day they'd shared. "Just tired, I guess," she replied, stabs of guilt poking her in the abdomen.

124

Kerry wiped her mouth with her sleeve. "When you guys were at the falls, did, uh, did Christian say anything about me?"

Leigh chewed the inside of her mouth. "Just that he's glad to be back and see you and stuff."

A curl of annoyance formed on Kerry's lip. "He's really starting to bug me."

"What are you talking about?" Allison asked.

"Just that every little thing I do these days is wrong, and everything he does is right." Kerry frowned. "He's on my back about studying, he thinks I've taken on too many activities. . . ." She shook her head. "He's acting like my dad or something."

"Really?" Leigh couldn't imagine Christian acting that way.

"And if he mentions jolly old England one more time, I'll puke all over the Paddington bear he gave me."

"Give me Paddy before you do that," Leigh said.

"You got it." Kerry blew her bangs off her forehead. "Maybe I'm being impossible, but all these little things annoy me. Like that earring he wears now. *Please.*"

"Better on his ear than his tongue." Leigh stuck out hers.

"Kissing a guy with tongue jewelry feels cool," Allison said knowingly.

"Gross!" Kerry and Leigh cried.

Allison grabbed Kerry's arm. "Don't look, but Dale Curtis and Victor Kowalski are checking us out."

Kerry and Leigh immediately turned and looked. Sure enough, the guys were staring straight at them.

When they saw they were busted, the guys laughed. Then they waved.

"Victor got really buff over the summer," Allison gushed.

"And have you seen how his rear looks in his football pants?" Kerry grinned wickedly.

"You were looking at Victor's rear?" Leigh whispered.

"I'm only human."

"But don't you, like, only have eyes for Christian?" Allison asked, her eyes wide. "You give all of us 'hook up on Thursday, break up on Tuesday' couples hope."

Kerry shrugged as they came around the bend toward Ms. Baker, quickening their pace a bit. "The way I'm feeling lately, I . . . I just want to keep my options open, that's all."

Leigh's and Allison's jaws dropped to the ground.

"Come again?" Allison asked. But Kerry was no longer by their side—with a sudden burst of speed she'd run ahead and left them in the dust. Allison turned to Leigh. "I can't believe she said that!"

"Neither can I," Leigh whispered.

And although they were barely jogging, Leigh suddenly felt as if her life were now speeding up at an amazing rate.

"You can't say that!" Leigh exclaimed on Wednesday night. Christian had come over after dinner, and they were holed up in the Feralanos' family room, putting the final touches on their project.

"Why not?" Christian leaned back on the couch,

126

grinning smugly. "If the facts show that I was a better parent than you were, I can't help it."

Leigh folded her arms across her baggy sweater. "What facts?"

"I put the key in Charlie's back every time."

"Me too."

"I kept a totally detailed journal of the experience," Christian continued.

Leigh waved her book in the air. "Got that."

Christian stared at Leigh, his eyes narrowing to a squint. "Did you sponge bathe and diaper Charlie?"

"No—but we didn't have to do that." Leigh's eyes narrowed too. "Unless you spilled something on him . . . or stained him with newsprint from the sports section."

Christian laughed, holding up his hands. "Guilty as charged."

Leigh smiled. "All right, then." She picked up her journal and flipped to the right page. "Now that we've established that we're on equal footing, let's go over the three personality traits we hoped Charlie would develop. I picked kindness, being responsible, and happiness. How about you?"

Christian moved closer, looking over Leigh's shoulder. He nibbled on his pencil. "Well, I had being positive, caring about the environment, and willingness to try new things."

"Those are good," Leigh said, trying not to feel his warm breath on her cheek. It had been hard enough not to notice his gorgeous smile and his irresistible laugh when he was on the other side of the couch.

"So are yours, but happiness doesn't count."

"Why not?"

"Happiness isn't a trait you're born with—it's something you have to go after. You know, the pursuit of happiness and all that."

"Well, *I* think it's a trait," Leigh insisted stubbornly.

"If it is, that would mean that you always do what makes you happy," Christian said. Leigh held her breath as he moved a fraction closer.

"Do you know what makes you happy?" Christian asked gently, his knee bumping lightly against hers. Leigh swallowed. "Sorry," he apologized.

"That's okay." Leigh took a deep breath, trying to relax. "Happy? Well, sure. Shopping, hanging with my friends—"

Christian shook his head. "No, happy in here." He put his hand on his chest.

Leigh's heart skittered back and forth as he came even closer. *Don't do this, Leigh. Quick, remember your other personality traits . . . like . . . like . . .*

Then shyly, nervously, and quickly, Christian leaned forward, touching his lips to hers.

For a moment Leigh forgot everything: She forgot that her mom was chatting on the phone in the kitchen, forgot that her favorite TV show would be on in a half hour, forgot that she hadn't taken a shower since gym class today. And she forgot all about kindness and responsibility.

All she knew was that she was sitting on her scratchy wool couch kissing Christian Archer for all she was worth.

Then she remembered. He was Kerry's boyfriend.

Leigh moved back, her heart thudding rapidly in her chest, her lips tasting of Chap Stick and Coke. Of her first *real* kiss. Of Christian.

How could I have done such a thing? she panicked. "I think you'd better go now," she managed to choke out.

Christian reached out to touch her shoulder, but Leigh scooted down to the end of the couch.

"Don't," she whispered. She was sure that at any moment she was going to cry. He had to go. He had to get out of there right this very minute. Because if he didn't, she might just let him kiss her again.

"Leigh, we need to talk."

"There's nothing to say." Leigh tried to busy herself by organizing the papers that lay scattered across the coffee table.

"Hey." Christian nudged her with his knee.

Leigh cleared her throat. "What's the big deal?" she said, knowing the words were absurd as soon as she said them. *What's the big deal about kissing Kerry's boyfriend, Leigh? Nope, no big deal at all.* "We just kind of got caught up in the moment, that's all."

"What moment would that be?"

Leigh lifted her eyes to meet his. Bad move.

He scooted toward her.

"The moment when two people who've been fighting an attraction for each other since the moment they first met finally give in and let themselves feel what they've been fantasizing about for weeks?" Christian asked softly.

"You've been watching too many talk shows or something." Leigh picked up a pillow and stuffed it in between them. *Wow,* she thought sarcastically. *That'll really keep him away.*

"Please don't close me out, Leigh. I've been so confused. I—"

"You're confused? How do you think *I* feel?"

For a long, agonizing moment Christian just sat there without saying a word. Then he picked up his books and stood up.

"Whether you admit it or not, you know I'm right. And I"—he took a deep breath—"I think you're the most amazing girl I've ever met," he finished, then ran upstairs.

Leigh sat motionless for a moment after she heard the front door close, then hurried up the two flights of stairs to her room. She flung herself across her bed and lay silently, feeling numb, for several minutes. Then she reached out to her dresser, picked up her handheld wooden mirror, and flopped down on her back, staring at her reflection.

Her lips were slightly moist and a bit swollen. Her heart-berry lipstick was gone without a trace.

She watched as tears began to slide down her face, not believing that she'd actually done it.

She'd gone ahead and kissed Christian Archer.

When the phone rang thirty minutes later, Leigh knew who it was before she answered.

"Hello?"

"Leigh, we've got to talk—"

"No," Leigh said, pacing the carpet. "There's nothing to talk about."

"But you know there is, Leigh. You know."

Fresh tears sprang up in her eyes. "I can't do this, Christian. I'm Kerry's best friend."

Christian sighed. "And you're a great friend. But the way I feel about you has nothing to do with Kerry."

Leigh closed her eyes so tightly that black and yellow puddles formed in her vision.

"Talking to you on the phone isn't going to work," Christian said. "Can I come back over and—"

"I don't think that would be a good idea. It's almost nine—"

"Please?"

"I have homework to finish," she lied, glancing over at her completed assignments on her desk.

"I need to talk with you. Not only about what happened between us, but about what's going on with Kerry." He hesitated. "Can you give me an hour or two? No strings attached. It'll just be a chance for us to talk. And if we decide that things aren't right, we'll have cleared the air between us."

"And if things *are* right?" Leigh asked, afraid to hear his answer.

"Then we'll go from there."

Leigh bit her lip, remembering how it had felt to kiss him. She knew she should say no. Meeting Christian could possibly be the worst decision she'd ever make. But the pleading in his voice and the desperation in her heart made her weak.

"On Saturday," she whispered. "But don't expect anything. I meant what I said."

"So did I."

After she hung up, Leigh realized that for the first time since she'd been new to Buffalo, she felt incredibly lonely. Who could she call to talk about things? Obviously not Kerry. And she couldn't very well call Lucy or Allison either. *Hey, guys. Guess what? I like Christian, and he likes me too. Isn't that wild?*

Sighing heavily, she wandered out into the hallway. She knew her dad was teaching his night class at the college. Leigh trudged down the stairs to the living room. She could hear the TV coming from below, a shaft of light spilling upward.

"Mom?" Leigh called.

Her mother, clad in flannel pajamas and fuzzy slippers, looked up from the scrapbook she was working on. It was a collection of photos from family vacations and birthday parties. They'd all been dumped into boxes when they'd moved, and Leigh's mom was on a mission to get them all into albums by the year's end.

"You're up late, honey," Mrs. Feralano said, patting the spot beside her on the floor. She touched Leigh's tear-stained cheeks, looking worried. "Is everything okay?"

Leigh curled down beside her. "Not really."

"Is it school?"

Leigh shook her head. A Halloween commercial for a local costume shop flashed on the TV. A

132

group of people dressed in various scary outfits danced around a fake bonfire. Maybe that was the answer—she'd spend the rest of the year wearing a mask to hide her sorry, guilty, lustful face. . . .

"Did you and Kerry have a fight?"

"No." Leigh bit her lip as a tear snaked its way down her cheek. "Not yet."

"What do you mean?" Her mom lowered the TV.

"Well . . . ," Leigh began, trying to find the right words to explain. "You remember Christian, Kerry's boyfriend?"

"Yes . . ."

Leigh's throat tightened. "Well, we, um, we kind of, well, kissed. Tonight," she finished, cringing as she said it aloud. She shot an ashamed glance at her mother.

But her mom drew her close. "And how do you feel about that?"

The tears began to slide fast and furious down her cheeks. "Like the world's worst friend." Leigh buried her face in her mom's neck. "Do you think I'm a terrible person?"

"Of course not." Her mom pulled away and lifted her shoulder up toward her ear. "My neck's all wet now, you."

"Sorry."

Mrs. Feralano pushed Leigh's hair off her face. "Is this the first time it's happened?"

"Yes!" Leigh cried.

Her mom nodded. "Do you want to tell me more?"

Leigh took a deep breath. "Ever since Christian's come back, Kerry's been telling me things are weird. That they don't quite feel like they used to."

"That's understandable."

"I know." Leigh sniffled. "And because of school and stuff, I've been spending a lot of time with Christian. And he's kind of been telling me the same thing as Kerry."

Her mom wrinkled her brow. "Sounds like those two need to talk to each other, not use you as the middleman."

"I know. . . ." Leigh picked up one of the photographs. It was from last summer's vacation to Rhode Island, where they'd spent the week touring gorgeous old mansions and eating insane amounts of fresh lobster and crab legs. Leigh smiled wistfully as she put it back down. Everything was so easy back then.

"So where does kissing you fit in?" her mom asked.

Leigh shrugged. "Christian told me that he's been having doubts about being with Kerry . . . and how much he likes me." She hesitated. "And I like him too, Mom. I even told him that I'd meet him on Saturday to talk about everything." Leigh lowered her head. "Say it. Say what a horrible person I am."

"If all you two did was kiss"—she gave Leigh a stern look—"and that better be all"—Leigh nodded anxiously—"then you didn't do anything wrong."

"You really don't think so?"

"No." Her voice grew serious. "You'll meet

Christian and you'll talk. But if you discover that the kiss you two shared was more than just the heat of the moment, then you've got to tell Kerry. That's the right thing to do."

Still blushing at hearing her mom actually say "the heat of the moment," Leigh nodded.

It was three days until Saturday.

Just three days to make a decision that could change her life forever.

Eleven

"HUTT, HUTT, HIKE!" Jason took the snap from center, pivoted, and handed the ball off to Christian, who started up the middle, then broke to the outside. Christian's breath came in slow, even gasps as he pushed forward, dodging fleet-footed Richie Perez, sidestepping chunky Al Van Aiken, the football clutched tightly in his grasp. When he was finally tackled, Christian rolled over onto his back on the cold hard sod of Baxter Park and stared up at the blue September sky.

"You all right, Archer?" Perez asked, extending a grass-stained hand and quickly pulling him to his feet.

"Yeah." Christian pushed up his sleeve and glanced down at his sports watch. "Let's finish this offensive series. Then I've gotta get going."

"Already?" Perez let out an exasperated sigh. "You're going to screw up the sides now." He gestured impatiently to the other eight guys.

136

"We've been here two hours already, man." Christian leaned forward, his hands on his thighs, his head down. "We'll give you one more offensive possession, and then that's it."

Jason loped over. "Don't sweat it, guys. My brother said he'd meet us over here around two, when he gets out of work. Then we'll be even again."

"Okay." Perez nodded to Christian, mollified. "Let's go." He jogged back to his group of teammates, who stood huddled several yards away, strategizing their next play.

After both sides had completed the agreed-on series, Christian said his good-byes, brushed the loose dirt off his old Buffalo Sabres sweatshirt, and jogged down the path toward home.

Baxter Park was only a few blocks from his house. There was the usual assortment of swings and jungle gyms for the kids and a large pavilion where concerts were held on hot summer nights. On autumn Saturdays you could always count on a game of tackle football to take place. The picnic tables that were clustered under the big oak trees near the pavilion were party central on the weekend, and come Monday morning, the park's large steel garbage cans would be filled with empty glass bottles and crushed beer cans.

Christian had come here with Kerry right before he'd left for his trip. Avoiding the loud, raucous laughter, they'd made their way through the trees until all they could hear was the occasional sound of a bat flapping in the branches above them. They'd held hands in the fading dusk, and Kerry had fought back tears as Christian had awkwardly told her that their year apart would be over before she knew it.

He knew what she'd wanted him to tell her—what she'd probably expected him to say, but he didn't do it. He couldn't. Even though they'd been together for a year, the words still sounded strange to his ears, and the thought of actually saying "I love you" made him feel kind of sick.

He hadn't been ready for a girl to be so into him back then, to think he was so cool, so great. And he didn't have a clue as to what love really was. Plus how could he say "I love you" when his palms still sweat every time they held hands and there was no doubt that Kerry could hear every double-time beat of his heart? Guys who were confident enough to open up like that to a girl weren't relying on cool-mint breath spray to get them through the night.

But now he was a senior. He could deal with a girl's feelings better. Saying those three little words to someone didn't seem so scary anymore.

To someone.

That was the kicker. Those words had to be said to the right person.

And at the thought of it, his palms started to sweat and his heart began to pump like crazy.

Most of the trendy shops that lined the Elmwood Strip were decorated for Halloween. Dried corn-stalks wrapped around lampposts, colorful banners of ghosts and goblins dangled from storefronts, and ghoulish jack-o'-lanterns ogled passersby from behind gift-shop windows.

Christian and Leigh had walked almost four blocks in silence, passing clusters of Buffalo State students and Saturday-afternoon shoppers popping into Sal's Kitchen to get a bottle of gourmet salsa or the Book Nook to search for a rare novel. Elmwood was one of Christian's favorite places in the city.

Leigh had barely looked his way from the moment he'd picked her up that afternoon. This was nothing new—she hadn't met his gaze in school all week. Ever since they'd kissed, she'd withdrawn into some kind of shell. He'd been worried that someone would pick up on her aloofness, but no one had. And when Kerry was around, he saw that Leigh made a real effort to be her usual self—though in his heart he could tell she was anything but.

Christian had told Kerry that he'd be playing football all day and would be hanging out at Jason's house afterward. He knew lying, even of the little white variety, was wrong, and he felt bad for doing it. But there was no other choice. He couldn't see Kerry today—not until he'd had a chance to talk to Leigh.

"Cool stores, huh?" he asked.

"Mmmm."

"Have you ever been over here?"

Leigh tucked her hair behind her ear. "Nope."

Christian stared down at the ground, his trainers caked thick with football mud. Each time he thought about what he was doing, his stomach twisted itself up into knots and unraveled again.

This afternoon wasn't about showing Leigh the sights and sounds of Elmwood or any of the other lame things he'd mentioned when she slid into his car. He was here to show her, well, himself.

Was he a terrible person? he wondered miserably. A liar? A cheat? The scum of the earth? *No*, Christian thought. *I'm just one confused guy.*

He and Kerry had gone to the movies yesterday. They'd held hands and kissed good night, but Christian had felt as if he were playing himself in a B movie and doing a bad job of it at that. Their conversations lacked spark, and worse, their kisses lacked passion.

Now he looked over at Leigh. "Feel like grabbing a burger or something?"

"No thanks."

Last night Christian had been so disillusioned that he'd sat down and made a list of traits that he looked for in a girlfriend. A good sense of humor. Intelligence. Looks. Warmth. Sensitivity. And as he'd kicked back in his swivel chair he realized that Kerry had all those traits. But that didn't do him much good.

Because if you had to make a list of what you liked about your girlfriend, you were obviously in big trouble. Guys in love didn't go around making lists of what they liked about their girlfriends—unless they were so confused about their relationship that they needed a list to remind them of what had attracted them in the first place.

"I'm not . . . in love with Kerry," Christian blurted out. A feeling of immense relief flooded

140

over him. To finally say it out loud felt so good. "It's not that I don't love her." He ran his fingers through his windblown hair. "But—"

Leigh's brown eyes were nonjudgmental. "But?"

Christian came to a stop outside The CD Exchange. "I don't feel like I used to. Like I want to."

"You just—just stopped loving her?" Leigh asked, her eyebrows lowering slightly. She looked so vulnerable right then. When he thought about what she was risking to even consider being with him, he realized how lucky he was.

"No." Christian shook his head. "It wasn't like that. I wanted things to work out with Kerry just as much as she did."

Leigh didn't respond.

He took a deep breath. "I wrote, I called—and she did too. Kerry was my connection to my life back here. My *old* life."

"A life you were starting to leave behind," Leigh said, a hint of sadness in her voice.

"Not just me—it was both of us. Kerry's changed too." Christian had lain awake last night, thinking about Kerry and what had happened between them. He'd come to the conclusion that they probably would've parted ways sooner if he hadn't gone abroad. They were good friends and had some great times, but they just weren't meant to be together forever. Maybe when you made a commitment at twenty-five, you could guarantee it would last. But at sixteen? Seventeen? It was so hard to predict. Who was to say that he and Leigh were meant to be forever? All he could count on was how he felt right now.

And how he'd felt since Wednesday night. "The kiss," Christian said awkwardly, leaning against a large oak tree on the edge of the sidewalk. "That made—"

Leigh wrapped her arms around herself. "I can't live with myself if I'm the cause of—"

"You?" Christian interrupted, shaking his head. "Of course not. How I feel about Kerry has nothing to do with you. No, it's just that . . . when I'm around you, I feel so good. And I—I want to be around you all the time."

Leigh's cheeks flamed a bright red. "But what about Kerry? She's my best friend. How can I hurt her like that?"

Christian gestured to a small wooden bench tucked among the trees. "Can we sit down for a second?"

With a resigned look on her face, Leigh complied.

"Do you think she wants to break up with me?" Christian asked.

Leigh opened her mouth, then abruptly closed it shut. "I'm not the person you should be asking. You guys need to talk to each other."

Christian knew she was right. Yet he hadn't been able to say any of this to Kerry. He was afraid. Would she cry? Yell? Scream? He swallowed. "I've been trying to talk to her. But it's hard," he said feebly, knowing he sounded like the wuss he was.

"Yeah, must be hard to talk to your girlfriend," Leigh said, uncharacteristically cold.

"That's kind of the whole problem," Christian

explained. This was not going well at all.

Leigh shrugged. "Maybe I gave you too much credit. I didn't think you were the type of guy to run away from commitment."

"I'm not!" he protested.

"What are you doing, then?"

"I just don't believe in committing to the wrong person. God." He stared up at the sky. "My friends, you—everyone's making me feel so lousy for feeling how I do. Like I'm the most rotten boyfriend in the history of dating."

A few long seconds passed.

"I know you're not," Leigh said at last. "You're entitled to be confused. You're a guy."

Pathetic, but true. He glanced over at Leigh, taking in her firm yet sweetly sympathetic expression. She was being tough with him, but he deserved it.

Leaning over, Christian kissed Leigh softly on the cheek. Her skin felt warm on his chilled lips, and the small shudder that passed through her body made him want to throw his arms around her and hold her forever.

But he didn't. Instead he pulled back.

"Why me?" Leigh's face was a mixture of emotions he couldn't read.

"Why you?" Christian repeated, confused.

Leigh scuffed her shoe in the dirt. "Okay, it's a given that I'm a terrible, horrible friend who's sitting here with her best friend's boyfriend as he tells me he's going to dump my friend for me. But why me? Why not some other girl?" A dull glaze settled in her eyes. "Am I just someone to step in on the rebound?"

Christian inched a little closer. "I would've broken up with Kerry whether or not I met you. It just worked out that we met before it happened . . . and now it's kind of messy." He swallowed, taking a moment to think. "I, well, I can really be myself around you," he said. "More than around anybody else."

Leigh ran her fingers through her wind-tangled hair. "Me too," Leigh told him. "Maybe you're right." Then she sighed. "Or maybe it's that I like you so much, I'm convincing myself this whole conversation makes sense."

Christian leaned back on the bench. "I'm going to break up with Kerry," he said at last. "And if you don't want to go out with me after I do, then——"

"Then I'd have to be crazy," Leigh said, turning her face to his and kissing him fully on the lips.

Christian wasn't sure what it was: the sound of oak leaves rustling on the sidewalk in front of them, the steady flapping wings of Canadian geese flying south overhead, or the way Leigh smelled of Johnson's baby powder when he kissed her.

All he knew was that he'd never been so happy—or so in love—in his life.

Twelve

"HAVE TO GET moving," Leigh mumbled. Yet even when the alarm went off after the fourth time she'd hit the snooze button, she couldn't manage to drag herself out of bed. A song Leigh loved was on the radio, and for a moment she closed her eyes, refusing to acknowledge the Monday morning sun that was creeping through her blinds.

And the guilt that was creeping into her brain.

Leigh kicked back the sheets and grabbed her pink chenille bathrobe from its hook on her closet door.

The cold tile bathroom floor sent shivers through her toes as she quickly pulled off her pajamas and hopped into the shower. Only now, in the privacy of her tiny bathtub, behind the plastic floral curtain, did Leigh allow herself to think about him.

Christian.

Was the conversation they'd had on Saturday a

dream? Had Christian really said those things to her? And had she really kissed him?

Leigh thought of how his lips felt on hers—tentative, but warm. Soft, but not without pressure.

Oh, yeah. I kissed him.

As she squeezed out some shaving gel she decided to look on the bright side of things. Kerry had not been happy since Christian returned. And Christian was definitely unhappy about the state of their relationship. It wasn't like she had anything to do with their breakup. *If anything, I've been trying to keep them together,* Leigh thought self-righteously.

But then her puffed-up virtuosity deflated. No matter how she tried to kid herself, she knew Kerry was going to be crushed when Christian broke up with her. *And then let's add an extra helping of abuse by telling her that Christian wants to go out with* me *instead.*

No. Leigh grabbed the razor and viciously mowed her legs, salty tears mixing in with the pulsing shower. The romantic fall afternoon they'd shared in Elmwood became a blur—a crazy fantasy she never should've made possible. No way. She might not be able to pick and choose who she fell in love with, but she could pick and choose who she went out with.

And it definitely wouldn't be anyone named Christian Archer.

"Do they really think they're fooling us by calling this sad excuse for a sandwich a pita wrap?" Lucy complained.

"I had the same thing for lunch the other day."

Allison picked up Lucy's sandwich, examining it with a critical eye. "In fact, that *is* the same sandwich I had the other day."

"Ha-ha. Just for that I'm taking one of your cookies."

Leigh tried to smile as she bit into her bagel, but inside, her stomach was churning. Would Christian really break up with Kerry? Kerry hadn't been in gym class this morning. Something about not feeling well, Ms. Baker had said, and sitting in the nurse's office.

"Did you hear that Will Kryski broke up with that girl he was seeing from Maryvale?" Lucy asked.

"He broke up with her last week," Allison corrected.

"Are you sure? I heard that . . ."

From the far doors of the cafeteria Leigh saw Kerry come in, head down, shoulders slumped.

And she knew.

Kerry walked quickly through the crowded cafeteria and dropped into the vacant plastic chair reserved for her next to Leigh, her green eyes rimmed with red.

"What's wrong?" Allison and Lucy burst out.

"Are you okay?" Leigh echoed, dreading the response. How could she have ever thought Kerry wouldn't be upset? Being with Christian had totally killed any rational brain cells Leigh had in her head.

Kerry's chin began to quiver. "Christian broke up with me," she whispered, her voice cracking with each syllable.

"Get out!" Allison exclaimed, dropping her fork.

"You're kidding." Lucy shook her head.

"I don't know what to say," Leigh said, her throat parched and dry.

"I called you, but your line was busy," Kerry sniffled to Leigh.

"My dad was on the phone with my uncle," Leigh explained. But no one heard her—they were all riveted to Kerry.

"Details," Allison demanded.

Kerry's eyes welled up with tears. "He called and said he wanted to talk, right?"

Leigh and her friends nodded.

"So then he comes over, and I asked him if he wanted to watch TV or something, but he said no, he didn't want to come in. So we sat down on my front porch swing, and he—he . . ." Tears began to spill down her face. "He told me that he didn't think we were right for each other anymore and that he thought we should see other people." Kerry started to hiccup.

"Drink this," Lucy ordered, thrusting her water bottle at Kerry.

"Man." Allison's eyes drifted over the male population in the cafeteria. "Guys. Did you have any idea he felt like that?"

Kerry took a few shaky sips. "Things have been kind of weird, but I had no idea he was going to break up with me."

"So, he just, like, told you he wanted to end it?" Lucy asked, picking a piece of tomato out of her pita and popping it in her mouth.

"Tactful, Luce," Allison commented.

"You guys have been fighting a lot lately," Leigh offered timidly.

"No, we haven't!" Kerry snapped, ripping open her lunch bag. Her normally pale skin was blotchy from tears, and her pug nose was bright red. "No more than anyone else does."

Lucy and Allison shot Leigh disapproving glances.

Leigh shrugged nervously. It was true! Well, maybe they weren't full-out fights, but Kerry had gone on and on about how they weren't getting along. Had she been the only one listening?

No one said anything for a few minutes.

"Do you think you guys can be friends?" Leigh tried again.

Kerry, Lucy, and Allison looked at her as if she had three heads. "Like that would happen in the real world," Lucy said.

"Well, at least he had the decency to tell you," Leigh said feebly. "Some guys wouldn't even do that."

"True," Allison said, her eyes narrowing. "Anyone remember Roger the Dodger, the guy from the mall? Three weeks of pure bliss, then no phone calls, no E-mails, and no signs of life." She shook her head. "And then when I confronted him, he said he didn't think I'd be upset." She swigged down the rest of her milk. "Loser."

"Some guys are afraid of commitment," Leigh added.

"All guys," Allison declared.

"Like that's an excuse." Lucy was indignant.

"At least I have friends like you I can count on,"

Kerry said, wiping her eyes. "You guys are always here for me."

Lucy and Allison nodded emphatically. "Best friends forever."

"Forever," Leigh echoed, giving Kerry a weak, watery smile. She felt like crying herself.

As she crumpled up her brown paper sack and brushed the crumbs from her lap, she knew what she had to do.

Her friendship with Kerry depended on it.

It wasn't hard to find Christian after school. If he wasn't practicing kicking drills with the soccer team in the gym, he'd be hanging out with his friends in the band room. Leigh opted for soccer. As she walked through the hallways, clutching her books to her chest, she rehearsed what she would say when she saw him.

Sure enough, he was heading into the gym, casually bouncing a soccer ball on his knee. For a moment she let herself imagine what it would be like to be his girlfriend: to keep his picture in her wallet, to share secrets each night before she went to bed, to hold his hand in the halls. . . .

But that wasn't going to happen. Leigh cleared her throat and called out to him, hoping that her presence outside the gym didn't raise any suspicious eyebrows. *Like I should be worried. These guys wouldn't know a girl liked them if she sent them a love letter signed in blood.*

"Hey." Christian jogged over, a smile lighting up

his face. An adorable, hard to resist smile. Leigh steeled herself against its charms. She had to. "How's it going?"

Leigh stared down at the dirty tile floor. "All right."

Christian leaned against the bank of lockers that lined the hall, shifting the ball back and forth in his hands. "I guess you probably heard."

"Yes."

"She was upset."

"That's kind of an understatement," Leigh said.

"I know. I'm upset too."

Leigh bit her lip. "She took it so hard—she came into the cafeteria crying."

Christian's smile had vanished—in its place was a look of incredible sadness. Leigh knew that Kerry was so angry right now, she'd rip Christian apart, but if Kerry could see his face, if she could see how torn up he was over this, she knew her friend couldn't hate him for long. How could she?

Christian shook his head in frustration. "I didn't want to hurt her."

Leigh knew that. Eyes like that couldn't hurt anyone.

"Girls always say they want guys to be honest. But then when you are, you end up doing more damage." He hit the ball against the lockers. "You know, my friends thought I should just blow her off. Stop calling and stuff."

"That would've been a swell parting gesture," Leigh snapped.

Christian sighed. "I'd never do that to anyone."

Leigh softened. "I know." He looked so forlorn, so forsaken that all she wanted to do was reach out and touch his soft, warm cheek. "Do you think you guys can be friends?" After the scene in the cafeteria, Leigh wasn't so sure. That kind of thing might happen in magazine articles, but as Lucy had said, real life was a different story.

"I'd like to think so."

Leigh couldn't get her feelings straight. One minute she was on her way down here all set to tell Christian she couldn't see him, and the next minute she was rethinking everything all over again. This was one of the hardest decisions she'd ever made in her life. Here she was, turning away from the first person she'd ever had major feelings for.

She liked him so much. What if she never met anyone else like him?

Then she had a worse thought. What if she never met anyone else like Kerry?

Leigh wrapped her fingers tightly around her spiral math notebook, the metal digging sharply into her skin. "Well, the reason I came down here was—"

"You mean it's not to watch me kick butt in there?" Christian joked.

"No." Leigh toyed with her necklace. "It's that . . . I can't go out with you."

"Leigh—" Christian moved closer to her.

Leigh shook her head, avoiding Christian's eyes. "I can't."

"But why?"

"You know why," she said, her voice dropping.

"But I would've broken up with Kerry anyway," Christian protested, his voice echoing throughout the near empty hall.

Leigh could feel herself crumbling inside, but she stood her ground. "That won't make Kerry feel any better."

"Archer! You coming or not?" A stocky blond guy Leigh vaguely recognized stuck his head out from the gymnasium doors. "We need you in here."

"I've got to go," Christian said helplessly, his eyes flashing to the gym, then back to her. "Unless you want to talk, and I can skip—"

Leigh swallowed. "No, I gotta go too."

"But the other day we had such a great time." He put his hand on her shoulder, his touch sending quivers down her back. Every ounce of her wanted to throw her arms around him, to feel the softness of his sweatshirt and his dark, glossy hair between her fingers.

"Kerry's my best friend, and she's hurting. I can't hurt her more by going out with you."

"Not now, then, but maybe in a few weeks," Christian suggested. "Or months, or . . ." His voice shook with emotion.

I can feel like this about someone else, she thought fiercely. *I can!*

"Don't you have anything to say?" Christian asked, his eyes pleading.

"There are plenty of girls to date at Fillmore," Leigh said, backing up. "Girls who aren't me." And then she turned and broke into a full-fledged run down the hall.

The rest of the week was a messy, depressing blur. Kerry's eyes lost that red-rimmed sadness, but Leigh knew that the pain she felt was just as sharp as it had been on Monday. And she could vouch from experience because the pain she felt at saying good-bye to Christian hurt more and more with each passing day.

Ever since she'd made her feelings clear, Christian had stayed out of her path. In fact, it seemed as if he was going out of his way to avoid her. She rarely saw him in the halls, and in health class he was polite, but nothing more. Now that they'd handed in their parenting assignments and received big fat A's, there wasn't any real excuse for them to talk to each other.

At times Leigh almost wondered if she were crazy, imagining the whole thing. Had Christian really had feelings for her?

Leigh was Kerry's shoulder to cry on, a willing listener, and all that a best friend could be. But at night, when Leigh lay restless in her bed, having a best friend wasn't enough anymore.

Yet it was all she had.

Thirteen

"*TIME IS ON my side, yes, it is,*" Mick Jagger crooned from the stereo speakers at Burger King.

"Yeah, right," Christian muttered, balling up his burger wrappers and aiming them for the trash. He should have known he'd miss the target. Nothing good was happening for him these days.

"Yeah, right, what?" Jason asked, dumping two sugar packets into his chocolate shake.

"That's so disgusting," Richie Perez said, then shoved three onion rings in his mouth at once.

Jason smirked. "You don't know what you're missing."

Oh, yeah, I do, Christian thought. It had been thirteen days since he and Kerry had broken up and twelve days since Leigh had told him to have a nice life without her.

Christian was at a standstill. And hanging out

with Jason and Richie wasn't giving him much in-spiration—neither of them had gone out with a girl for longer than a month. As much as he valued their friendship, they weren't really much help to him now.

It was messy, liking someone who was friends with someone you used to date. Once you went out with a girl, there was some sort of unwritten rule that you couldn't date any of her friends. Friends were taboo. Verboten. Prohibited under all circumstances.

Even beautiful, black-haired, California-raised circumstances like Leigh Feralano.

Christian couldn't stop thinking about her. Leigh was in his thoughts during school and in his dreams at night. He had to rely on memory, though, because he'd avoided seeing her as much as he could. If he saw her, then he might end up smiling at her. And if he smiled at her, then he'd probably say hello. And if he said hello, they'd end up having a conversation . . . and, well, it was obvious where that would all head.

Avoidance at all costs.

"Are you going to stop bumming out or are you going to walk around looking like a lost puppy all year?" Jason asked.

Christian tried to smile. "Ruff. Ruff."

Richie let out a deep, rumbling burp. "You'll meet someone else."

"I know."

"Besides," Jason put in, "it's not like Kerry's

sitting around all weepy for you. Victor Kowalski gave her a ride home yesterday."

"What are you, a spy?" Christian asked, annoyed. But he'd noticed himself that Victor and Kerry were hanging out together around school quite a bit.

"Just thought you'd be interested."

At first Christian had thought that Kerry was just trying to make him jealous. Maybe at first she was. But the expression she had on her face when he saw her with Victor wasn't fake—he could tell. He'd felt kind of down about it at first but then was genuinely glad for her. And hearing about her with Victor now left him feeling strangely unemotional. Probably because every ounce of emotion he had was tied up in thinking about Leigh.

"You guys about ready?" Richie asked. "I gotta get home before Sasha tears the house apart." Richie's Yorkshire terrier was known to have a serious temper problem when left indoors for too long.

Christian dumped the rest of his trash in the garbage. "You know what you said about meeting someone?"

"Yeah," Jason said, standing up.

"There is a girl at Fillmore who I like."

"Who?" Richie and Jason asked in unison.

"Leigh."

"Leigh?" Jason repeated. "You and Leigh Feralano?" Richie whistled. "Trouble . . ."

"What's wrong with Leigh?" Christian bristled.

"You didn't just ask us that," Jason said.

157

"Remind us who her best friend is." Richie scratched his chin thoughtfully. "Some blond girl."

Christian scowled. "Shut up."

Richie chuckled. "Besides that, does she even know you exist?"

"Once that health project ended, she got as far away from you as possible," Jason said.

Christian pushed open the glass door. "Yeah, well, it's kind of intentional. She doesn't want to hurt Kerry's feelings."

"Maybe you've just got wicked BO," Richie commented.

Jason zipped up his coat. "So, how long before you ask her out?"

"I already did," Christian said. "She turned me down."

"Ooh, cold," Jason said.

"Ice princess from California."

Christian shook his head. "Nah, she's cool. Just loyal."

"Well, if you're really into her, maybe you need to show her. Don't take no for an answer," Jason suggested.

Christian thought for a moment. Maybe waiting, hoping she'd come around *wasn't* the thing to do. Maybe Jason was right.

Maybe it was time to let Leigh know how he really felt about love.

He started out slowly, with little things he hoped would please yet not offend her: a Post-it note stuck inside her locker, asking that she give him a chance. A brief message on her answering machine, asking the same thing. And then, the most romantic thing he could think of—a small pumpkin painted on both sides with a happy face and a sad face, along with the photograph of them from Niagara Falls in a plain wooden frame.

None of it worked. She didn't return his phone call, she didn't acknowledge the pumpkin or the photo, and if she'd received the note, she never said a word.

So Christian threw himself into soccer, studying, and his friends. And it was okay. But it wasn't great.

He could survive without a girlfriend—heck, he'd done it for a year. But he didn't want to now.

Christian Archer knew what he wanted.

He wanted Leigh.

The mall was fairly crowded, so it was easy to slip into the Sweater Set unrecognized. Except for the heavyset salesclerk who smiled flirtatiously at him when he walked in, no one gave him a second glance.

Leigh was standing on a ladder attached to the wall, arranging sweaters in a colorful wall display. Her hair was piled into a disheveled bun, and she had on a cute pair of jeans and a lime green turtleneck. A vision in merino wool.

Christian waited until a few nearby browsers moved out of the way, then sidled up beside her. "Hungry?" He held out a bag of tantalizingly warm cinnamon buns. "Still hot from the oven."

Leigh gasped. Whether it was from shock or pleasure, Christian couldn't tell.

He opened the bag, releasing the warm, spicy scent. "I'd give you one now, but they're kind of sticky. I might have to wait until you're through with your shift."

Leigh hopped off the ladder, shaking her head. "Don't do this."

"Do what?" he asked. "Bring a friend a cinnamon bun?"

"You know what I mean." She glanced nervously out into the mall. "Someone might see you."

"That would be awful," Christian deadpanned. "Imagine the scandal. Boy brings girl peace offering in shape of cinnamon bun."

Leigh's lips curled into a grin in spite of themselves. "Can't you see I'm working here?"

Christian pulled a bright red tunic from the rack. "Do you have this in my size?"

"And what size is that?"

"Well, it's for my girlfriend—actually the girl who I hope will be my girlfriend. Maybe you can help me out. I'm not quite sure what her taste is."

"She hates sweaters," Leigh came back at him. "Try the jeans store down at the other end of the mall."

Christian dropped the tunic and moved toward her. "Nah, I think she likes sweaters. She's just afraid to wear them, that's all. She's afraid that the other girls in school won't like her or something. But that's not true."

160

"Christian . . ."

He put the bag on the ladder. "Why won't you return my calls, Leigh?"

"You know why."

"It doesn't make sense," he said. "Kerry and I are history."

"I can't." But her voice softened.

Christian put his hands on her shoulders and stared into her eyes. "I want to get to know you," he pleaded. "Please, give me one good reason why you won't give me that chance."

Leigh ducked out of his grasp and turned away. "Because you have an ex-girlfriend named Kerry Cole."

"So what do you think?" Kerry pulled out a black turtleneck sweater and black leggings from her closet, tossing them on her bed next to a pair of orange-and-black-striped tiger ears and a matching tail.

"It's the cat's meow," Leigh teased. She was sleeping over at Kerry's tonight, and for the past fifteen minutes she'd been sitting cross-legged on the floor of Kerry's room, trying to brainstorm an idea for a Halloween costume.

"Have you come up with anything?" Kerry asked, turning up the radio.

Leigh shrugged. "What do you think of an easel?"

"An easel?"

"I'd wear white tights and a white leotard and maybe hang an easel over my shoulders covered with paint."

"You could always hang out in front of the deli

161

and advertise lunch specials if the costume's a bust."

"Very funny." Leigh racked her brain for some other ideas. A fifties greaser? A harem girl?

Kerry swept the clothes off her bed and sprawled out. "I'll be so glad when this semester's over and we don't have health anymore."

Leigh braced herself for the inevitable attack against Christian. Or maybe it would be praise. She was never quite sure what would come out of Kerry's mouth. But it would be passionate. Over the past few weeks Kerry had talked endlessly about him—his good points and bad points and points in between. Leigh had listened to it all with the patience of a saint. And she'd never mentioned a word about what had gone on between her and him.

Not that her silence meant her feelings had changed. Sure, she'd told him to stay clear of her. But she hadn't meant it. Not really.

Leigh was a sucker for romance. A romantic card. A small gift. A visit just to say hi. And Christian had done all three. She was nuts to even waste a second. The guy was perfect for her. Yet every time she heard Kerry rail against him, she knew she'd done the right thing.

"Yeah, because I told Victor I'm taking ethics next semester—and now he is too."

Leigh's jaw dropped. "Say what?"

Kerry grinned. "Victor Kowalski? The basketball forward? He's taking ethics with me next semester."

"Victor, as in cute blond band guy with the great you know what?"

"That's him." For the first time in almost three weeks Kerry's eyes were full of sparkle.

Leigh gulped. "Does this mean that you're over Christian?"

Kerry stared up at the ceiling. "I don't know. Almost." She rolled over onto her stomach. "I know I'm not as angry as I was." She grinned sheepishly. "And after all the complaining and moaning I've done, you're gonna kill me, but I'm actually hoping Christian and I can still be friends."

Leigh sat up on her knees. "Kill you? I think that's great!"

"It was crazy to expect him not to change."

Leigh nodded.

"And I realized that I've probably changed since last year too. We've grown apart."

"So you're okay about it now?" Leigh whispered.

"Yeah. Funny enough, I guess I am." Kerry picked up Fred, her stuffed turtle, and played with his stubby turtle legs. "If Christian doesn't want to be with me, I've got to accept it, as much as it hurts." She pointed to the Fillmore High pennant on her bulletin board. Stuck underneath it was a scrap of notebook paper with Victor's number on it. "And move on."

Leigh leaned over and gave Kerry a huge hug. "It's so good to hear you say that," she said, practically choking up from joy. Goose bumps did the cha-cha down her arms.

Maybe she *would* have a chance with Christian after all.

*   *   *

For once Leigh was glad about having to stay for Monday afternoon study hall. She had her French workbook open to today's assignment, but even the easiest vocabulary words garbled together in her brain.

She'd been over the situation a million times in her head: Kerry and Christian had broken up. Kerry had told her she was over him. While it would be kind of weird to date someone who'd been so important to Kerry, Leigh felt so right about Christian—so sure that they would be perfect together—that any icky thoughts were quickly pushed aside.

She took a deep breath. It was now or never.

With a quick glance Leigh got up and headed to the front of the room, making sure to walk two aisles over and straight past Christian. But it didn't matter because he didn't even look at her. Which wasn't unusual—ever since last week at the Sweater Set he'd avoided her as if she were the plague.

The note stuck to her sweaty palms. Her sneakers squished noisily on the linoleum. Mr. Simms eyed her suspiciously from the front of the room. Her plan was failing before her eyes.

"Just sharpening my pencil," Leigh explained for no reason at all, quickly performing the task. She turned and headed back to her seat, eyes downcast.

Do it, do it, do it.

With a quick flick of her wrist and a feigned look of nonchalance she dropped the note on Christian's desk, then walked back to her seat as fast as she could.

A flood of emotions gushed through Leigh as

164

she watched Christian open the note. Excitement. Nervousness. Happiness.

And cold, pounding fear.

At two-forty Leigh stood on the front school steps, smiling at people as they left for the day, backpacks over shoulders, earphones blasting.

"Have a good evening!" Abigail Sundquist called over her shoulder as she hurried past Leigh.

"You too," Leigh said, trying her best to look casual.

If he doesn't come, it's no big deal, Leigh told herself. *I'll get over it. So what if I just gave him the most soul-revealing note of the century?*

Leigh had spent a good hour composing her letter last night. After several tries and lots of balled-up papers she finally got down what was really a simple message: Christian was the first guy who'd ever made her feel special, and she couldn't keep pretending that she didn't feel anything for him when she felt *everything* more intensely than she ever had in her life.

She wanted to be with him—if he still wanted to be with her.

"Yo, Leigh, want a ride?" Jason called from the parking lot.

She chewed her lip, stealing a look inside the huge glass doors that led to the lobby. She'd been standing there for almost ten minutes now, and there was no sign of him. It wasn't as if the school were that big a place. He should've been here by now. And he'd rushed out of study hall before she'd had a chance to speak with him, giving her no indication that her heartfelt words had struck any kind of chord at all.

"Um, well . . ." She moved toward his beat-up Mustang. "I guess—"

"Where do you think you're going?" Christian asked, materializing by her side. He thrust what appeared to be a hastily composed bouquet of wildflowers in her face. "Sorry I'm late—those fields behind school are farther than I thought."

Leigh looked back over at Jason, who had slid behind the wheel. "I don't need one after all," she called, barely suppressing the overwhelming happiness building inside her.

Jason grinned back at them. "So I see."

"So."

Christian had given her a ride home, and they'd been sitting on her front steps for over an hour now, sometimes talking, sometimes not, watching the occasional car drive by.

"I really like you, Leigh."

"I like you too." She turned her face to his, the warm sun tickling her cheeks.

"I don't want to, you know, rush you into anything," Christian told her, his fingers gently lacing through her hair.

"No way," Leigh whispered, inclining her head toward his.

And then they were kissing.

When they pulled apart after a few seconds, Leigh couldn't keep the ear-to-ear grin off her face. "I'm really glad you like me."

Christian laughed. "And I'm really glad you like me back."

Leigh leaned her head on his shoulder. "But—"

Christian knocked his head lightly against hers. "No buts."

Leigh giggled. "Okay, no buts. It's just that we need to tell Kerry. Before we're—you know, together."

"You're right." Christian picked up an acorn and threw it, aiming it for a small red maple tree. "She should hear it from us."

"How do you think she'll take it?" Leigh asked.

"She's been spending a lot of time with Victor K., from what I've seen," Christian commented.

"Yeah, she likes him," Leigh said. "And he's called her a couple of times."

"Oh."

Leigh shot a cautious glance at Christian. "You're not jealous, are you?" she asked, fear nibbling in her stomach.

"Not at all." He leaned over and kissed the tip of her nose. "I'm really happy for her. I never wanted to see her miserable. And besides, how can she have a problem with us, then?" Christian put his arm around her, nuzzling her head with his temple.

Leigh snuggled close. *Christian's right,* she thought. Kerry couldn't get mad about this. She was totally over Christian. Besides, she'd wanted Leigh to find a special guy.

And after almost sixteen years of waiting, she finally had.

Fourteen

"It's going to be fine," Christian assured Leigh as they rounded the last corner before Kerry's house.

Leigh nodded mechanically. She'd thrown up her wheat toast and cereal only seconds after eating this morning. Last night had been long and horrible, filled with tossing and turning. The minutes that she did spend asleep were filled with images of Kerry and Christian and herself—none of them smiling, all of them scary.

Today was the day.

The day that would make her the happiest girl in the world or the sorriest one on the planet. No matter how many times she'd rationalized the situation and no matter how many times she'd told herself that Kerry had moved on, the thought of actually telling her that she and Christian were a couple made her queasy right down to her toes.

As if reading her mind, Christian patted her hand. "Trust me. How can she be mad?"

Leigh shrugged. People were crazy when it came to love. Even though Kerry was over Christian, it didn't mean she'd be happy to hear that he liked Leigh.

Suddenly they were at Kerry's house. Leigh had called Kerry to ask if she wanted to go to the fall festival that was being held in the park—when Kerry said she wasn't sure if she could get the car, Leigh told her that Christian had mentioned going and that maybe they could catch a ride with him and his friends.

Kerry had paused for a moment. "Sure. Why not," she'd said finally. "Got to start this friend gig sometime."

Leigh stared out the window at Kerry's house and unfastened her seat belt. "Trust me," Christian repeated, his words ringing hollow in her ears.

Kerry was standing in the middle of a bunch of leaves, raking like a madwoman. Leaves were flinging everywhere.

"I think the idea is that they go in the pile," Leigh kidded, getting slowly out of the car. Her smile felt frozen and fake.

Kerry laughed. "I spent the past half hour raking them into a nice, orderly pile, and when I did, I couldn't resist jumping in them. Call me crazy." She turned to Christian. "Hi."

"Hi."

Leigh chewed the inside of her lip. No hostility. This was a good sign.

"So where's everyone else?" Kerry asked, squinting

at the car. "Maybe they want to come in and have a drink or something before we go. I think my mom got some apple cider."

Leigh paused, taking a deep breath. "No one else came," she said, forcing her voice to be cheerful. "It's just us."

"Jason and Paul couldn't make it?" Kerry asked, pulling out some leaves that were stuck in the rake. "Guess floral swags and woodcrafts aren't really their shtick, huh?"

"We, um, we didn't ask them," Christian spoke up. "We wanted to talk to you in private about something."

Kerry rested her cheek on the handle of the rake. "You sound so serious."

"Well, it's, um, it's kind of funny, actually." Leigh laughed nervously. "I, uh, I finally met someone who I really like. You won't believe—"

"Don't tell me it's Jason." Kerry broke into a triumphant grin. "I *knew* you guys were perfect for each other. Sure, he's a big lug, but when you finally—"

"It's me," Christian said, cutting her off.

"What?" Kerry asked, the traces of her smile melting away.

"It's not Jason that Leigh was talking about," Christian explained. He took a deep breath. "It's me, Ker. We . . . we—"

"Excuse me?" Kerry spoke in clipped, measured syllables.

"We wanted to talk to you first," Leigh rushed out. "That's kind of why we're here—"

"You've got to be kidding." Kerry's voice was low, and her hands clenched the rake so tightly, her knuckles blanched.

Leigh froze, stricken. She'd never seen Kerry look like this before.

"Tell me this is some episode of *The Twilight Zone*."

"We hoped you'd be okay with it," Christian said nervously.

Leigh looked anxiously at Kerry. "After what you said about Victor and everything, well, well . . . ," Leigh stammered. This was a disaster. "You know, I just thought that you wouldn't—"

Kerry's mouth tightened up into a horrified little scowl. "The two of you? *Together?*" She looked from Christian to Leigh, then back to Christian again.

Leigh reached out to touch her. "It's not like we planned to like each other," she tried, knowing her words were ineffective the moment she said them. "We—we, just, I—"

"Shut up," Kerry said.

The words hit Leigh like a slap.

"Kerry—" Christian started.

"Just shut up!" Kerry burst out, tears welling up in her eyes. "I never want to hear anything either of you have to say again!" Before Leigh could stop her, Kerry had spun around and run up the front porch and into the house. The door slammed shut.

For a brief moment Leigh thought she was going to pass out right in the pile of dead leaves. Leaves as dead as her friendship with Kerry.

Christian's face was ashen. "Should we give her a few minutes and then ring the bell? Maybe she'll calm down."

"No. Trust *me* this time. That wouldn't be a good idea." Leigh turned on her heel and walked quickly back to the car. What kind of fool had she been? So what if Kerry and Christian had broken up? He was her first true love. Seeing him with another girl had to hurt. A tear rolled down her face. *And when that other girl was me . . .*

"I can't believe we did this," Leigh whispered as Christian got into the car.

"I didn't think she'd react so badly." Christian rested his head on the steering wheel.

Leigh pulled a leaf from the bottom of her shoe and threw it angrily out the window. What a jumbled, tangled mess they'd made. "No matter what you're thinking right now, we did the right thing," Christian said as he pulled away from the curb. "Kerry will come around."

But Leigh knew his voice sounded much braver than he could have felt inside. She noticed that his right hand trembled on the steering wheel.

Girls didn't have the monopoly on suffering—guys could hurt just as bad. But Christian hadn't just suffered the biggest loss of his life, Leigh realized, staring out the car window.

He hadn't just trampled on the heart of his very best friend.

Fifteen

"COLE! IF I have to tell you one more time to watch that stick, your butt's going to be warming the bench in my office after class." Ms. Baker glared at Kerry and blew her shrill whistle again.

Leigh clutched the worn wooden handle of her hockey stick and faced forward, leaning expectantly over her knees. She'd dreaded coming to school today after what had happened the day before. At first she'd debated feigning some sort of debilitating illness, but she knew her mom probably wouldn't buy it. Besides, that would look like she was afraid to face Kerry.

Which, of course, she was.

And facing her across the dirty gym floor in a game of indoor hockey at 9:40 A.M. was not the way she wanted to start the day.

There were six girls on the Reds, six on the

173

Blues: a goalie, a center, and four sides, two of whom could travel. As luck would have it, Kerry and Leigh were on opposite teams, and each was a traveling side. Kerry had been playing with a vengeance and had already been called twice for fouling Leigh with her stick. She hadn't actually hit her, but she'd lifted her stick way over the height limit, something that Baker despised.

Each time she was near Kerry, Leigh tried to catch her eye—to smile, to plead. But all she got was a cold, hard glare and fierce determination.

At the sound of the whistle Mary and Ashley, the two centers, faced off, and the puck slid across the floor toward Leigh. She smacked it with all her might, shooting it to the other side of the gym. Leigh raced forward, a rush of resolve propelling her sluggish legs toward the goal. She was getting weary of shouldering such heavy emotions—fear, sadness, love. She'd never felt so many things in her life, and they were all happening at once without the security of a good friend to confide in.

By the time she'd arrived at school this morning, the news about her and Christian had spread like wildfire. Leigh knew Christian hadn't said anything, and she guessed that Kerry had probably just told Lucy and Allison, which meant that the entire junior class would be in on it by lunchtime.

"So we can become an official couple now," Christian had said with a half smile, dropping by her homeroom before first bell.

"Yeah," Leigh had responded. Being a couple

was the last thing on her mind. While the thought of being with Christian still sent shivers up her spine, every time she looked at him, she remembered the stricken look on Kerry's face and she felt horrible all over again.

Allison and Lucy had told her they definitely didn't want to take sides but that they thought Kerry was overreacting. Leigh had really appreciated their support, but she didn't want to get into a who's right, who's wrong debate with her friends. Besides, what did it matter what other people thought?

And here in the gym it was pretty apparent what Kerry thought.

Leigh took a deep breath and cleared her head. Ms. Baker always told them to leave their problems outside the gym and not let them interfere with their performance. There'd be plenty of time today to worry about things with Kerry. Right now all she wanted to do was release some steam.

When Ashley sent the puck flying to meet her wide-open stick, Leigh stopped it and began to run, pressing nearer and nearer the Blue goal.

Just as she was getting ready to smack it toward the net Kerry's red stick blocked her. Wood battled wood as the two girls vied for the puck. Kerry managed to hit it just right and the puck sailed past Leigh, back toward her own goal.

Instead of turning and running, though, Leigh hesitated. Now wasn't exactly a good time to talk; still, she could try.

But as she opened her mouth Kerry sped past

her. "Can't steal everything away from me," she called over her shoulder.

So much for leaving her problems outside the gym.

After that excruciating forty minutes was up, Leigh hurried back into the locker room and practically flew into an ice-cold shower. Then she pushed her way back to her locker and began to get dressed. As she pulled her shirt over her head she could feel someone next to her. She didn't even have to look. "I thought you were my friend," Kerry said, her voice low.

"I *am* your friend," Leigh said, pulling on her blue wool tights.

"No, you're not," Kerry said. She yanked on her leather boots. "A friend doesn't go after another friend's boyfriend. A friend doesn't steal guys."

"But I didn't," Leigh protested, a surge of injustice welling up inside her. Here she'd tried so hard to avoid hurting Kerry, and none of it mattered. Kerry hated her anyway.

"You were probably hot for him the moment you saw him," Kerry accused, her voice growing louder. "And I was such a dope, running to you, telling you how *worried* I was. How I didn't think things were the *same*." She looked derisively at Leigh. "And you were laughing all the way to Christian's cheating little arms."

"That's so not true." Leigh pulled on her skirt and sat down on the locker-room bench.

"And I so don't believe you," Kerry said sarcastically, fumbling for her makeup kit. She pulled out a tube of lipstick, her fingers shaking.

"Kerry, please. Can we not get into this here?" By now several girls from gym class had gathered around. They were pretending to get dressed and put away their things, but Leigh knew they were watching—waiting for something to happen.

Kerry shook her head. "It's amazing how you can think you know someone and *boom*. They do something like this."

Leigh took her books from the gym locker. "You're not being fair!" Beads of cold sweat began to form on her forehead. "You aren't in love with him now. You told me so yourself. It . . . it just happened, Kerry. You were telling me how you liked Victor, and, well, I'm sorry if I misunderstood," she finished in one big gulp. "I don't know what else there is to say."

Kerry's face crumpled, causing waves of guilt to wash over Leigh. "Ever since you came here, you've been nothing but a good friend. I just never expected you'd turn on me like this."

"But I'm not! I didn't!" Leigh cried, putting her hand on Kerry's shoulder.

Kerry recoiled from her touch as if she were poison. "Well, it sure looks that way to me." She turned and fled from the room, her soles slapping against the hard tile of the locker-room floor.

Leigh stood there, clutching her gym bag. Then slowly she picked up her books and walked out of the smelly, cramped girls' locker room, avoiding the speculative stares of her classmates. Leigh knew the truth even if no one else did.

She hadn't stolen Christian from anybody. He'd been there for the taking.

But what good did being right do if no one believed you anyway?

As if gym class hadn't made her hate life enough, she'd been so out of it that morning that she'd forgotten her sack lunch on the kitchen counter, as well as the two extra dollars that would've let her afford the overpriced salad bar.

The price she had to pay for her forgetfulness?

Tuna casserole.

"Thanks," Leigh mumbled as the cafeteria lady ladled a generous helping onto her plate.

She was already halfway to her table when she stopped suddenly. What was she thinking? She couldn't sit there.

Lucy, Allison, and Kerry were already eating. Leigh's chair sat empty, mocking her.

Leigh took a faltering step forward, then glanced quickly around the noisy cafeteria. Where else could she go? There was no way she would sit by herself. *If I hadn't already got this stupid tray full of food, I could've snuck out of here with no one noticing,* she thought.

Should she try to sit with them? She'd already managed to survive one heated exchange today. Maybe with Allison and Lucy there to back her up, it wouldn't be so bad. Maybe Kerry would be calmer now.

Just then she caught Lucy's eye. Her friend hesitated slightly, her expression flustered. Leigh smiled, then shrugged—as if to say she understood.

"Mind if I sit here?" she asked Abigail Sundquist, who was sitting with a few other girls Leigh vaguely knew.

"Sure, go ahead," Abigail said, scooting over.

When Leigh glanced over at her old table a few seconds later and saw Kerry's backpack sitting comfortably on her chair, she knew she'd made the right decision . . . for once.

Sixteen

"SEE THIS BUILDING?" Christian pointed to a photograph. There were so many things he wanted to share with Leigh, so many things he wanted to tell her about.

Leigh sat next to Christian on the Archers' carpeted living-room floor. "The Tower of London, isn't it?" She reached into the huge ceramic bowl for a handful of freshly popped popcorn.

"Mmm-hmmm. And that's where the crown jewels are kept. You know, that big heavy crown with the purple velvet inside that sits on the queen's head when she's making some la-di-da appearance? Princess Diana wore some of the jewels that are kept there too. Necklaces and tiaras and stuff."

"Wow. I'd love to see those," Leigh said, munching.

He thumbed quickly through the thick pile of glossy four-by-sixes. Leigh had promised to help him make a big scrapbook of his trip, but for now they were just going through the pictures.

"Check out the size of this bird." It was a raven, pecking at some crumb on the ground. "Tower legend has it that if the ravens fly away, the Tower of London will crumble. Probably a tourist gimmick, but the beefeaters—the guards at the tower—are real protective of the ravens."

"And for good reason." Leigh studied the picture carefully, taking in every detail and sending little jolts of happiness into Christian's heart in the process.

Being with Leigh was incredible. Christian found himself walking by her classroom just to get a glimpse of her cute little face scrunched up in thought. He called her on the phone way too much, he knew, but the sound of her voice and the melodious sound of her laugh tickled him like nothing ever had. And nights like this, where they just hung out at his house or with friends and enjoyed each other's company, were the best of all.

Leigh tickled his ribs. "You're a good photographer," she told him.

Christian propped himself up on his elbow. "Maybe I can take a picture of you, then. Since you won't give me one yourself."

She blushed. "I'll give you my class one when they come in. *If* it's good."

"If it's of you, I know it will be," Christian said, kissing her softly on the lips.

More than two weeks had passed since he and Leigh had become "official," but he knew she was still having a hard time adjusting. She'd told him over and over again how much she missed Kerry, how lonely it was going through the days without her to laugh with.

Christian missed Kerry's friendship too, but not in the way Leigh did. And lately Kerry seemed to have warmed to him. No longer was she shooting him dirty glances or, worse yet, walking by as if he weren't even there. She'd even said hello to him in the hall the other day.

Christian had told Leigh he'd do anything she wanted to try and make things better between her and Kerry. But Leigh had been adamant about his staying out of it. This fight wasn't about Christian anymore, she'd said, and maybe it never had been in the first place.

It was about the boundaries of friendship.

After Christian drove her home, Leigh took a nice long bath, plucked a few stray eyebrow hairs, and made some final touch-ups to an English paper that was due tomorrow. Then she kissed her parents good night, took out her thin red marker, and carefully drew a big red heart on her wall calendar in the square for that day. She'd started doing this when she and Christian began going out, and already half a month of hearts had passed.

Empty hearts, though. Empty because she didn't have a best friend to share this wonderful, exhilarating experience with.

Leigh still couldn't get used to the fact that she

couldn't just call Kerry up and ask her to spend the night, or rent a movie, or laugh over some dumb thing that had happened that day. And she couldn't get used to the fact that she'd had to change her daily routine at Fillmore: Now she ate lunch regularly with Abby, Sunny, and Monica, caught up briefly with Lucy and Allison in the halls, and tried to avoid passing by places she knew Kerry would be.

Leigh took off her pink bathrobe and hung it up on the plastic hook inside her closet. Of course some things were easy to get used to: funny notes and goofy "thinking about you" presents from Christian, hanging out with him and his friends after school, talking to him for hours on the phone every night. All that was easy—and just what Leigh had always hoped for in a relationship.

But some things are much, much harder to deal with, she thought as she crawled under the covers. Like going to an FHS basketball game to root for Jason and seeing Kerry look straight at her without acknowledging her presence. Or walking through the halls before Thanksgiving and hearing everyone talk about their holiday plans and wondering what Kerry and her family were doing. Being the tenth instead of the first to find out that Kerry and Victor were going out.

Kerry had perfected the cold shoulder treatment perfectly.

Christian had been really sweet and concerned, but she didn't want him to interfere. This was her problem.

Before she'd had a boyfriend, Leigh used to lie in bed at night and wonder about what it would be like when—and if—she ever did.

Now she lay in bed thinking of the guy of her dreams—and a friend who was fading farther away with every new heart that appeared on the wall.

Seventeen

LARGE, FLUFFY DECEMBER snowflakes fluttered past the dining-room window as Leigh sat at the smooth oak table writing Christmas cards. She was wearing a fuzzy green sweater and ankle socks covered with little reindeer, and each fingernail alternated between shiny red and green polish. She'd hoped that if she dressed in the Christmas spirit, somehow she'd *feel* it too.

But she was just going through the motions today and every other day for the past week. She'd baked candy-cane cookies with her mom. They'd hung their big wreath on the front door, the tiny white lights twinkling out as if to say hello to the matching one that hung on the Chapmans' door across the street. And she and her dad had picked out a beautiful Douglas fir.

Now Leigh breathed in the wintry scent of pine and tried to start writing. But nothing was coming out right. What was she supposed to say? *Dear Aunt*

Carol: Merry Christmas! Thank you for the new top you sent me for my birthday. By the way, I stole my best friend's ex-boyfriend just in time for the holidays. Happy New Year! Love, Leigh.

The doorbell rang then, startling her.

"Leigh, can you get it? I'm trying to get this computer program to run," Leigh's dad shouted from his office.

"Okay!" Leigh yelled back, pushing away from the table.

She hurried to the front hallway, her ankle socks slippery as she slid down the linoleum foyer. The sight that greeted her when she opened the door stunned her.

Kerry stood on the front porch, shivering in her green parka.

"Kerry. Hi."

"Hi."

"Uh . . . come in." Leigh stepped back.

Kerry followed Leigh into the house. Leigh's mind whirled through a thousand thoughts as she watched Kerry struggle to remove her snowy wet Timberland boots.

"Here, I'll take your coat," Leigh said, reaching out for the parka. After she hung the coat in the closet, she just stood there, staring at Kerry like a dolt.

"Guess you're surprised to see me," Kerry said, a lopsided grin on her face.

Definite understatement of the year. Leigh nodded. "I don't know what to say."

"Can we sit down or something?" Kerry asked.

"Sure," Leigh rushed out, flustered. "I—I made some cookies yesterday. The candy cane kind you gave me the recipe for last year."

Kerry laughed, holding out a small, tinfoil-covered pie plate. "Here's some more for your collection."

"Oh, thanks," Leigh said, clutching the plate and staring at it as if it were the crown jewels on a silver platter. "This is the nicest Christmas gift I could've gotten."

"They're just cookies."

"I know," Leigh sniffled as they entered the living room.

"Look how pretty your mom decorated in here," Kerry said, admiring the Dickens village set up on the coffee table and the mantelpiece draped in garland.

Leigh nodded. "She worked really hard."

"It shows." Kerry sat down stiffly on the couch.

Leigh dropped down too.

Kerry took a deep breath. "You know how we have that big Thanksgiving dinner at my house, with all my aunts and uncles?"

"Sure," Leigh said, wondering where this was leading to.

"Well, every year we all go around the table and say what we're most thankful for. You know, things like health and doing good in school, stuff like that."

Leigh nodded.

"It was funny because I hadn't even been thinking about what I was going to say, but when it was my turn, I suddenly blurted out you."

"Me?" Leigh squeaked.

"You. 'Leigh,' I said. 'My best friend, Leigh.' And I've been thinking about it ever since."

Leigh shook her head. "But why would you say something like that?" she asked, the muscles in her face beginning to quiver. "I'm the person you hate."

"No, you're not," Kerry said, a catch in her voice. "I'd never hate you."

"You could've fooled me."

Kerry sighed. "I was so angry when I found out you liked Christian. I felt like the two people I trusted more than anyone in the world had gone behind my back."

"It wasn't like that," Leigh whispered, her voice husky. "The more time I spent with Christian, the more I started to like him. But I never would've acted on my feelings if you hadn't told me how you guys were growing apart. We never, ever wanted to hurt you."

Kerry ran her fingers over the roof of one of the little village houses. "I know."

"I never wanted to hurt you in any way," Leigh said, a tear running down her cheek. "You've got to believe me. It just hasn't been the same without you in my life, Ker."

"Me either," Kerry said, fighting back tears as well. "And I was so mean and cold to you, and you didn't deserve it."

"Yes, I did," Leigh protested. "I deserved every mean thing you said."

"No." Kerry shook her head. "Christian and I were a breakup waiting to happen. And sure, maybe

I wish he'd picked someone else to fall in love with besides you. But when I see you guys together, I can tell how right you are for each other."

"Really?" Leigh said, wiping her nose on her sleeve.

Kerry nodded. "I know in school I've been acting like I don't notice you at all, but I have, and I"—she began to cry—"I've realized how happy you two are together and how miserably I handled the situation."

Leigh threw her arms around Kerry, burying her face in her hair. "I missed you so much."

"I missed you too."

Leigh pulled away. "Promise we'll never fight again, okay?"

Kerry grinned through her tears. "Promise."

Leigh sank back in the couch in a happy, dazed shock. "There's so much we have to catch up on," she said, not knowing where to begin.

Kerry showed off a gold pinkie ring on her finger. "Victor gave me this last week," she said shyly. "We're going out now."

Leigh touched the ring's delicate heart, then looked straight into Kerry's bloodshot eyes. "I know in school that *I've* been acting like I haven't been noticing you at all, but I have, and I think you and Victor are perfect for each other."

Kerry raised an eyebrow. "Didn't you tell me that once before about someone else?"

Leigh blushed down to her toes.

Kerry laughed. "I'm kidding." She fingered the

ring. "I really like Victor, but I'm going to be a lot smarter this time. No more putting all my energy into a guy. That was a bad, dumb move." She took Leigh's hand. "I've had a lot of time to think over these past few weeks. I'll always have a soft spot for Christian—he was my first boyfriend. But we needed to let each other grow up and see what it's like to be with other people. I'm glad we broke up. And I'm glad he has you." She paused. "And I'm glad I have you too."

"Kerry?"

"Yes?"

"Would a double date be too weird?"

Kerry grinned. "Not to me."

Leigh grinned back. "Me either."

"No, no, no. You've got to put the lights on first. Then the ornaments."

"And tinsel too if you go for that look."

"And the star on top."

"Star? You mean angel."

Leigh looked at the festive scene around her and laughed out loud. There was Christian, a furry red Santa Claus hat on his head, opening boxes of ornaments and crunching on candy canes. Kerry was busy trying to untangle a particularly pesky string of blinking white lights. And Victor was passing out cups of Mrs. Feralano's hot mulled cider, manning the crackling hot fire they'd started in the fireplace, and looking at Kerry as if she were the brightest present under the tree.

190

Santa Claus didn't need to come this year—as far as Leigh was concerned, she'd gotten everything she could have ever dreamed of. A boyfriend, a best friend, and a new friend.

Christian touched Leigh's arm. He'd opened a small white box and had carefully unwrapped its contents.

Leigh peered over his shoulder to see, planting a tiny kiss on his ear. It was the handblown glass ornament Kerry had given her last year. Two little angels held hands—above their heads in script floated the words *Best Friends Forever*. Christian handed the ornament to Leigh. "This one's for you to hang up."

"For us," Kerry corrected, pointing to an empty branch. Leigh gently draped the ornament's slender gold string over the branch.

"Perfect," the girls declared in unison.

"How about I man the cider while you do the lights?" Kerry asked Victor, holding out her tangled web.

He grinned. "How can I refuse?"

Leigh smiled as the new couple sat down under the half-decorated tree branches and began to work together.

Then Christian drew Leigh toward the fireplace. "Now that we're really together, the pressure's on to get you just the right gift."

The fire's heat couldn't stop the shivers of excitement from coursing through Leigh's veins. "You don't have to buy me anything, you know. Having you is enough."

"Oh, no." Christian kissed the tip of her nose. "You deserve something really special."

"*This* is really special."

"Merry Christmas, Leigh," Christian said, reaching down to kiss her. "I hope all your dreams come true."

She snuggled into him, the soft beat of his heart thumping against her own. "They already have."

Do you ever wonder about falling in love? About members of the opposite sex? Do you need a little friendly advice but have no one to turn to? Well, that's where we come in . . . Jenny and Jake. Send us those questions you're dying to ask, and we'll give you the straight scoop on life and love in the nineties.

DEAR JAKE

Q: *Even though I was totally in love with my boyfriend, Joe, I broke up with him because I got scared about being in a serious relationship. Then I realized that I was being silly, and now I'm trying to get him back, but he says he's scared I'll just hurt him again. How can I convince him that won't happen?*

KF, Phoenix, AZ

A: There's no way you can promise Joe that you'll never hurt him again because no one can predict the future. When a relationship is first beginning, it's easy to make—and believe—those kinds of promises, but now that you've hurt Joe once, he knows it's possible and can happen again. However, even though you can't swear your undying loyalty just yet, you *can* try to make him understand that what led you to break up before had nothing to do with how much you love him. If you explain that you were afraid and needed time to sort out your feelings and that now you know you are ready for a big commitment, maybe he'll feel better about getting close to you again. Joe just needs some reassurance that you're not going to keep going back and forth, and once he sees you're not playing around, he should be willing to get back together.

Q: *I know I sound like a major dork, but I have to ask this question anyway. In my school everyone seems to be in cute little couples. Everyone except for me, that is. I'm sixteen, and I don't have a boyfriend yet. Is there something wrong with me?*

AG, Tampa, FL

A: I had to answer your letter because I receive so many other ones just like it. So I want all of you readers to know that there is *absolutely nothing wrong* with not having a boyfriend, okay? Each of you should know how many other girls out there are in the same boat and worrying about the same thing.

You know how some babies take their first steps months before other babies do? Just like with any other life event or serious responsibility, people are not all ready for relationships at the same point in their lives. Your friend might have been primed for true love at the age of fourteen, and you're still not there yet. We all work on our own schedules, and it wouldn't be fair to judge ourselves by what other people are doing. And even if you do feel like you're all set for a serious relationship, maybe you haven't met the right guy yet. I can guarantee some of the girls around you are settling for the wrong ones just to have boyfriends. That seems pretty pointless, doesn't it? Stick to your own timetable, and quit thinking that whether or not you have a boyfriend says anything about who you are.

DEAR JENNY

Q: *My friend Sheila and I both liked the same guy for a while, and it almost seemed like he was going to end up with her, but now he's been asking me out. She told me I shouldn't go out with him because he's a jerk who treated her badly and will probably do the same to me. I don't know if she's telling the truth or if she's just jealous because he chose me. Should I trust her?*

RM, Griffin, GA

A: Fighting with a friend over a guy is *the worst.* I've been there. And it's true that you have to doubt the one person who you're used to having as your total ally because suddenly she's not on your team anymore. But before you jump to the conclusion that Sheila's lying to you out of her own self-interest, you have to consider a few things.

First of all, do you know any of the details of

what went down between her and this guy? Ask her for the scoop, and then ask him for his side of the story. Any major gaps should clue you in to the fact that one of them isn't being honest with you. How long have you known Sheila, and how close are you to her? If she's a very good friend and you've never known her to lie before, she might be truly looking out for you. If not, take her advice with a grain of salt and find out for yourself what the guy's like. Remember also that just because things didn't work out between the two of them doesn't mean that he isn't right for you.

Q: *I know that Todd is my true love and that we'll end up together someday. But right now I feel like I want to date other people to know what it's like because this could be my only chance to have the experience. I just don't feel like I'm ready to be in a totally serious relationship yet. I don't expect Todd to wait around—I think he should date other people too. But what if when I'm finally ready to be with him, he doesn't want to be with me anymore? What should I do?*

RD, Lyndhurst, NJ

A: Your question is very tough. You're at one of those famous crossroads in your life when you have to make a decision that you'll always look back at, wondering what could have been. In the end you're going to have to trust your instincts and do what feels right to you *now* because predicting the future is a futile game. But I can give you some tips on how to make your decision.

Don't commit to Todd if your heart isn't fully in it. I understand that you're afraid of losing him later, but you can't let that influence what you do now if you don't feel right about it. You won't be happy with him, and there's still a good chance that you'll lose him because you'll start to resent him for keeping you from doing what you wanted. On the other hand, if the only reason you want to date other guys is that you feel like you *should*, and you're already convinced that you'd rather be with Todd and could be happy with him right now, then don't give that up.

Do you have questions about love? Write to:
Jenny Burgess or Jake Korman
c/o Daniel Weiss Associates
33 West 17th Street
New York, NY 10011

Don't miss any of the books in *Love Stories*
—the romantic series from Bantam Books!

You'll always remember your first love.

Looking for signs he's ready to fall in love? Want the guy's point of view? Then you should check out the  series. Romantic stories that tell it like it is— why he doesn't call, how to ask him out, when to say good-bye.

Nothing's worse than having to spend every day with someone you hate . . . unless you hate the thought of spending even one day without him.

Who Do You LOVE?
Janet Quin-Harkin

SUPER EDITION
Daring.
Irresistible.
Totally necessary.
Meet Rob Barden.

It's Different for Guys
Stephanie Leighton

I wanted to be with Will every minute of every day. Then I got my wish.

24/7
Amy S. Wilensky

For more edge-of-your-seat suspense,
read the bestselling novels of

LOIS DUNCAN,

author of *I Know What You Did Last Summer*